I0524460

Patrick Everard was born in 1967 near
Bournemouth on the South coast of England.
His debut novel 'Manila Boy' was published by
Book Guild Publishing, Brighton in 2010.
He currently lives in the Philippines, where
his interests include red wine and napping.

Also by Patrick Everard

'Manila Boy'

Blue has sold up his London flat and gone to live in Manila, vibrant capital of the Philippines - home to hustlers, ladyboys and a notorious criminal underworld. Blue desires sex and adventure, and very quickly he seems to be getting both... by the shovelful. But there are complications, and unwittingly he is being drawn into a very dangerous world, beginning with the complex Sidney Hamilton. A former West End actor. Who now spends his time idling between the Philippines and Thailand on his yacht, enjoying a cocktail of rentboy's and martinis. Is there a more sinister side to this charming rogue, and furthermore, what is Sidney's relationship with the menacing Geordie? A mountain of a man, and as hard as nails. Life on the streets of Manila has little value and as events start to turn sour it could ultimately lead Blue to tragedy.

RETRIBUTION

Patrick Everard

For Sajid

As my friend Paul constantly advises me - 'What you should do Patsy is........' Meanwhile Little Janie curls up on the sofa, shaking her head in disapproval, in-between mouthfuls of cake and vino.

1975

The V8 Jensen Interceptor pulled out of Wardour Street onto Old Compton Street, its 7.2 litre engine effortlessly accelerating past the 2i's Coffee Bar, famous for its live music from the likes of Cliff Richard, Tommy Steele, and Screaming Lord Sutch. Past Gerry's Wine and Spirits and the Golden Goose Amusement Arcade, scene of club owner Alfredo Zomparelli's bloody shooting the previous year, which Ronnie Knight, the ex-husband of Barbara Windsor, was purported to be behind. The 400 horsepower reined to a halt outside Club Bohemia, the pristine aqua turquoise paintwork emblazoned by the afternoon sunshine. The driver turned off the ignition, and as he opened the door, revealing a rich interior of cream leather, navy-blue piping, and dark walnut, the dying sounds of David Bowie's 'Ziggy Stardust' strumming out from the 8-track stereo could be heard.

A hand-stitched, Italian leather ankle boot stepped out of the car onto the kerb, followed by another as the driver gracefully slid out of the low coupe. An observer might have expected a far clumsier exit from a man so big, the Savile Row tailored suit barely constraining the 6 foot 3 inch, 220 pound powerhouse. The Spaniard, or The Hammer, depending on whether you were on his Christmas card list or not, stood looking up and down the street, checking for traffic wardens. Those who knew him as a friend called him The Spaniard, a name he had acquired due to his family background. His

Spanish father had joined the communist movement as a young man and had fought on the side of the Republicans at the outbreak of the Spanish Civil War in 1936. The following year, General Franco's Nationalist army gripped two-thirds of Spain, and his father had fled on a ship from his hometown of Bilbao, arriving in Southampton port in late 1937. Shortly after, he found work as a porter in Billingsgate fish market in East London and settled down with a lovely Irish girl, with whom he had a baby boy. That boy grew up to be known as The Spaniard, even though he was born in Deptford, and didn't speak a word of Spanish. But he did inherit his father's olive coloured skin, and smouldering Latino looks.

Those who had the misfortune of crossing him, of which there were many, knew him better as The Hammer, a nickname whispered in the corners of smoke-filled bars or on the shadowy streets of the East End, after two Turks who had tried to muscle in on one of his porn operations had come unstuck. Their bodies were found a week later bludgeoned to death down a back alley in Whitechapel. The police couldn't get the charges to stick, and not for the first, or last, time, The Spaniard walked free from Bow Street Magistrates Court.

After noting no wardens, The Spaniard tossed the keys of the Jensen to one of the two heavy-looking doormen standing outside the club. 'Only move it if you have to, Terry, and don't leave your paw marks all over the paintwork again.'

'Yeah, sorry 'bout that, boss. Won't happen again, boss.'

'Too fuckin' right it won't, Tel-Boy,' The Spaniard muttered as he slipped past Terry into the foyer of the club.

'Afternoon, Peggy,' The Spaniard greeted the old gal hoovering the floor.

'Hello, pet,' Peggy replied. 'He's in his office if you're looking for Harry,' she shouted over the noise of the vacuum cleaner. 'Probably having a hair of the dog, the silly old git. Got himself in a right state last night. Drank a bottle of your best cognac. I don't know why you put up with him, pet, I really don't. I would have thrown him out on the street a long time ago, but I know it's nothing to do with me, I'm just the dogsbody round here. Don't pay no attention to me, pet, I know my place.'

The Spaniard unplugged the hoover, causing Peggy to look up from her efforts for the first time since he had entered the club. 'Now what you gone and done that for? I got to get this finished and get out of here, I'm having' me *barnet* done down Raymondo's salon at six. A girl's got to look her best, even if she is just a skivvy. Me and Betty are going down the bingo tonight.'

'You look just fine to me, Peggy. Now, how about you take a break from all this hard work that you do and make us all a nice cup of *Rosie Lee*?' He then pecked her on the cheek and sauntered up the staircase to the manager's office, leaving Peggy huffing and puffing behind him.

'Hello, Harry, you got a hangover?' he asked the rather sallow-looking manager.

'What she been saying? That gossiping old hag should mind her own business,' replied Harry.

The Spaniard laughed. 'Come on, H, you're not exactly looking your best. How much did you put away last night?'

'Yeah, so I overdid it a bit, but it was medicinal, my nerves are shot to pieces. Those bloody heavies were back in again. You have to do something about it. Can't we just pay them, get them off our backs?'

'Which heavies?' The Spaniard interrupted.

But Harry was in full swing now, needing to get it off his chest, unable to halt his diatribe. 'It's me that's taking the flak here. Bloody Tweedledee & Tweedledum out there on the door think it's an open house. What's the point of having bouncers if they let any Tom, Dick, and Harry in here? I had two of those big Brummie bastards pinning me down on my desk last night, making it very clear that if we don't stump up some readies, next time I go to scratch my testicles, I'll have to fish them out of the bloody Thames first.'

Harry paused for breath, and could now see The Spaniard's face turning to stone. He knew better than to rant and rave at The Spaniard, but those two thugs had really put the wind up him. He also knew The Spaniard would never give in to any violent threats, particularly those demanding protection money. He would take care of it in his own effective way. But why was he being so slow in dealing with this? It was the second time these heavies had been in. You could guarantee the third time would be when they smashed the place up. Normally any sign of trouble and The Spaniard would nip it in the bud straightaway. And once The Spaniard nipped your bud, you would be enjoying a long spell in casualty. There hadn't been any trouble for over a year now. The old faces knew better than to cause a ruckus with The Spaniard, but suddenly this gang from Birmingham had appeared. A new gang trying to grab some of the London action. Harry and The Spaniard had never heard of them before, so maybe it was fear of the unknown that was preventing him from acting. In times gone by, you always knew who you were up against. Usually their reputations preceded them.

During the 1940s and 50s Billy Hill operated in the West End, and Jewish Jack Spot and his boys took care of the East End. They were well-known hardened crime bosses, demanding protection money, and organising high-level robberies. Then came the Italian gangs headed up by Albert Dimes, and soon the three were all competing for the same territory. The 60s arrived with the emergence of the Krays, who started muscling in on Jack Spot's manor, and the Richardson Brothers ruled south of the river. During that time the police were often as crooked as the villains. This went right through the ranks, from the beat officers upwards. Many were on the take, turning a blind eye in return for a bung. To continue operating, the pornographers, and the illegal drinking and gambling clubs not only had to pay protection to the crime bosses, but on top of that they would have to pay bribes to the cops. As long as the filth got their cut, things were allowed to run smoothly. Sometimes a raid was unavoidable. After all, the police had to be seen to be doing their jobs. But prior to the raid, those involved would be given a nod – a quick tip-off, that is – as long as they had made a charitable contribution to the police pension fund.

But things were changing now. It was the mid 70s and gone were the days when London was carved up and ruled by a handful of violent gangland bosses, with the police taking a slice of the pie. By 1969 the Krays had been made an example of and sent down with no prospects of ever being released. And both the Richardson's were serving long sentences at her majesty's pleasure, for extortion and assault. There was a new police commissioner, and a big reshuffle was going on throughout the Met, with many senior officers being given early retirement. That was not to say there weren't a few naughties still going on, and the odd palm still received a large dollop of grease. There were still criminal gangs in operation looking for protection money from bars and clubs. But they had learnt not to be so high profile. The criminal element and the showbiz crowd had always partied together. Actors were often fascinated by the murky underworld and the characters that operated in it. And in return, the villains loved nothing more than being photographed next to some star of the silver screen or a famous boxer. Often the criminals were searching for celebrity status of their own, but the first sign of that nowadays and the powers that be came down hard and stamped it out. It didn't do to let these thugs gain a cult image.

The Spaniard had been running Club Bohemia for eighteen months now. Inevitably, at the beginning there had been those who thought they could try it on with him and made demands, but they were soon dealt with in a very public and brutal manner. Very quickly the word went round to leave well alone. Even when he had a spot of bother with the local nick, his wildcard in the Flying Squad - DCI Eddie Mullins, came to his rescue and things were soon smoothed out. But now this, now some toe-rag from the Midlands was stepping well out of their territory, taking fucking liberties!

'Sorry,' Harry muttered quietly. 'Didn't mean to push it. It's just that these blokes really scared me. Maybe I'm getting too old for all this. Maybe it's time you retired me off. The sex joints are bringing in a handsome profit, and Pinky can take care of those for you now, he don't need me babysitting him any more. I'd like to get out of London, go and put my feet up by the coast. Me and the missus can spend more time with the grandchildren.'

The Spaniard cooled and sat down opposite Harry, waiting for him to finish. He crossed his legs and smoothed the immaculate trouser crease with one hand before lighting a Rothmans Royal with a chunky gold Dunhill lighter. There was silence between them as The Spaniard looked thoughtfully at Harry and took four long puffs of his cigarette.

'It's OK, H, I will take care of this,' he said softly. 'I promise you those clowns will never set foot in here again. You know I would never allow anything to happen to you. Have I ever put you at risk? You know me far better than that.' He paused, allowing his mind to wander. Maybe I have been too wrapped up in my own personal problems recently, what with Maggie and everything. But I guarantee by the end of next week it will all have been resolved and life will be back to normal. In the meantime, get Shotgun Charlie on the blower, I'm sure he'll enjoy a little jaunt up to Birmingham.'

2005

The club was heaving with half-naked, sweaty bodies, grinding away to Bob Sinclair's 'Love Generation'. Pepe and Samir were up on the balcony staring down at the arm-waving, euphoric crowd below.

'Whoa! Look at the jubblies on that!' Samir squealed with delight as one of the top-heavy girls dancing below swung her arms a little too frantically, and out flopped her left tittie from the scanty little vest she was wearing.

'Tart!' was the rather flippant response he received from Pepe.

Samir laughed. 'Oh, come on, it's not that bad in here. Chill, man, take a pill, let's party, baby!'

'You have got to be kidding? What are we doing in this place Sambo? I ain't going to get myself a nice bit of cock in here. Look at them, bunch of turgid breeders, can't even dance properly.'

'Alright, alright, Dorothy. Keep your wig on. You may have forgotten, but it's my birthday, not yours. And we are having a straight night tonight, remember? Now stop your moaning and swallow this.' With that, Samir popped a little orange pill into Pepe's mouth.

The E tasted rank on his tongue, and Pepe gulped down a couple of swigs of lukewarm lager from his plastic pint cup. 'Well, seeing that it's your birthday, I suppose I could make an effort,' he laughed, winking back at Samir. A hot prickle of excitement surged through his head, the thought of the Ecstasy speeding through his nervous system enhanced his mood almost immediately.

An hour later, Samir, grinning from ear to ear, was on the podium shaking and strutting between two twenty-year-old Essex girls. Pepe was shirtless, manically dancing next to a good-looking Manchester lad called Jack, who just forty-five minutes earlier had also dropped an E. And now in the overriding buzzing onslaught that riddled his body he had misplaced his girlfriend in the crowd, and was blissfully floating on the dancefloor near Pepe. The pill was having quite an effect, sending Jack's emotional happiness accelerating through the roof, and now this man Pepe, who he had never met before, was his newest, best friend in the whole wide world, and nothing else mattered.

Half the crowd on the dancefloor had taken something. There was always a good supply of drugs available from the usual dodgy geezers. Once upon a time, the management of the club tried to enforce a no-drugs policy, but the high sales of bottled water over the bar proved that the punters were still pill popping. So the owners decided to turn it to their advantage. The dodgy geezers flogging the pills were now working for the club. Any new faces coming in and trying to sell gear were soon escorted out the back, given a little slap from the bouncers and sent on their way. Now with the extra revenue generated from selling E's, and trebling the price of their bottled water, the management were laughing all the way to the bank.

Pepe felt the warm tingle spread through his body. The volume of the music seemed to be getting louder and louder in his head, the bass vibrating through him. The dance-track felt like it was tailored to his exact movements. Every beat, every note, seemed to be in harmony with his exaggerated Jagger-style moves. But then, whenever he looked at the good-looking

Manchester lad – whose name he'd forgotten already – dancing in front of him, the music seemed also to correspond perfectly to his much more sedate, flowing, hip and hand motions.

'Mmm… wouldn't mind giving him a bit of hand motion myself,' thought Pepe, smiling at Jack. 'He's a bit of alright.'

Another twenty minutes later and Jack's girlfriend had turned up. Pepe wasn't exactly sure whether she was actually dancing, or just giving Jack a right good bollocking. Yep, the more he watched, the more he was certain she was finger pointing and not waving to the music. Jack couldn't stop smiling, but it was obvious his girlfriend was far from happy, having spent the last hour having her backside repeatedly pinched and slapped as she fought her way through several stag parties looking for him, only to find that he was off his tits and couldn't stop grinning at her. After watching her empty her pina colada over Jack's head and then stamping on his toe, Pepe decided he might need to find a new dancing companion, and went in search of his mate Samir.

It was now 4.30am and the club had thinned out considerably, the party revellers having made their way out onto the chilly London streets, weaving and laughing their way to Trafalgar Square to catch a night bus, or queue for deliciously satisfying burgers, kebabs, and pizza slices near Leicester Square. Samir and Pepe were still in the club, straining every last ounce out of a great night. They had danced solidly for the last three hours. Samir had got the phone numbers for both the Essex girls. Not that he needed both, he was pretty sure they would come as a pair, the dirty little trollops. And now he was chatting up some drunk, chesty brunette, who had lost one of her shoes and spilt her vodka cranberry down her tight white top. This didn't seem to bother Samir much. In fact, in fairness he probably hadn't even noticed, he was so engrossed in his chatter with her.

Pepe was alone, a few feet away leaning on the bar, happy in his own little world. Watching the last few people on the dancefloor, he was coming down off the pill now, but still felt a lightness, a state of calm and pleasure. He wanted to go home and get into bed, but he didn't want to be alone in that bed.

'Hey! Hey!' Samir was calling him. 'Come over here,' shouted Samir, as he frantically beckoned Pepe.

'This is Bianca. Bianca this is my best buddy Dorothy.' Samir chuckled as he introduced the two of them.

'That's a funny name,' Bianca slurred, trying to steady herself on the nearby pillar. 'Why are you called Dorothy?'

'I'm not,' said Pepe. 'My name is Pepe, but Sambo just calls me Dorothy.'

'Hang on, hang on, who's Sambo?' Bianca asked. Then she looked at Samir's beautiful big black smiling face. 'Oh!' she grinned, 'that must be you,' hiccuping, and playfully poking Samir in the stomach at the same time.

'Yes,' he said, 'but my real name is Samir, not Sambo.'

'Oh blimey, it's so confusing, isn't it?' said Bianca, letting out a snort as she giggled away.

'Not really,' said Samir and Pepe in unison, glancing at each other.

'Lightning, this one!' Pepe muttered to Samir.

'Let's try again,' said Bianca. 'So you are Samir, and you are Dorothy. Or no, no, you're not, you are something else, but I've forgotten.'

'I'm Pepe, but Sambo here calls me Dorothy because I'm a knob jockey.'

'A what jockey?' Bianca asked, looking even more confused now.

'You know? A knob jockey, a pillow biter, a chutney ferret, a turd burglar,' Pepe said, trying to explain.

'A chutney turd?' Bianca squealed. 'How awful!' Then she fell into fits of laughter.

'No, I'm not a chutney turd,' Pepe frowned. 'I'm gay, a bit light on my feet.' And as if to prove the point, Pepe then broke into a little tap-dance. 'A poofter, yeah?' he continued.

'Oh right, now I get you,' Bianca smiled. 'Just like my little brother. He's a right little mincer!'

'Really? A gay brother? Is he as bright as you?' Pepe gave Samir a surreptitious smile.

'Yeah, he's got two GCSEs – French and Drama,' announced Bianca proudly.

'Mmm… very useful,' Pepe nodded in earnest. 'Is he planning on being the next Marcel Marceau?'

Bianca looked bewildered. 'Nah, he's crap at painting. Here he comes now. Hello, trouble,' she said to a nice-looking skinny lad, about twenty-one years old, coming towards them from the dancefloor.

'Hi,' he said, brushing his sweaty long fringe to one side, revealing a very cute face.

Pepe was all smiles. 'Ding dong!' he announced to Samir.

'Easy tiger, he's only a young'un,' warned Samir.

'I know, but what a cherub.' Pepe grinned.

'Where are you going now?' Samir asked them.

'Back to my flat in Streatham,' Bianca replied. 'Why? You wanna come back for something hot?' She winked at Samir.

The brother, slightly embarrassed by his sister's boldness, smiled shyly across at Pepe.

'I think I do,' Pepe said, slipping an arm around the brother's shoulders.

'I'm gagging for something,' said Samir, cupping Bianca's left hooter and giving the *raspberry ripple* a quick squeeze.

'Oi! What you doing?' She looked at him with a raised eyebrow.

'Oops… sorry,' Samir replied. 'But if your heart is as soft as your breast, I'm sure you will forgive me,' he grinned.

'If your cock is as hard as your hand, I will,' she squealed.

The four of them then rolled out of the door laughing, and Pepe hailed a black cab.

Samir turned to Pepe. 'Pretty cool birthday, bro!'

'Oh yes, indeed, Sambo, and now I think we're about to have cake!'

1975

The Spaniard took a table at the back of the pub where he couldn't be overheard. He sat sipping his pint of Double Diamond, watching the door. Fifteen minutes later, a tall, skinny fellow with a mop of unkempt, wiry ginger hair walked in, his weasel eyes shifting round the pub till they settled on The Spaniard in the corner. He ordered another two pints of DD and sat down opposite him.

'Cheers!' he said, raising his glass to The Spaniard.

'Hello, Charlie, welcome back. So how did the Midlands trip go?' The Spaniard asked.

'Fuck me! You don't waste no time, do you? Can't a man take a pull on his pint first?' Charlie smiled, but The Spaniard didn't return the gesture.

Shotgun Charlie was ten years The Spaniard's senior, not just in age, but in respect amongst the criminal fraternity. He had done two stretches in Parkhurst for armed robbery, hence the name Shotgun Charlie, and was widely known to have murdered Mick the Greek over a poxy poker hand. A violent temper and a couldn't-give-a-fuck attitude towards the law made him someone that most people either avoided, or trod on eggshells when around him. That was with the exception of The Spaniard, who wasn't, and never had been, scared of anything or anybody in his life, especially a gobby, lanky streak of piss like Charlie.

Shotgun Charlie looked into the cold depths of The Spaniard's shark-black eyes. 'Yeah, well, whatever,' he said, taking another sip of his pint, but lowering it quickly, so as not to push his luck too far.

'So tell me what happened?' The Spaniard continued coolly.

'OK. Well, there's this geezer up there that's done a couple of blags with me in the past. He knows who the big players are, and what they're into. He reckons the fella's that came down here and harassed poor old Harry work for a certain Arthur Connelly. Now, he's a top name in the Midlands, they don't get any bigger than this bloke. He's known as King Arthur up there. He owns several bars and clubs, plus he's got the gambling scene sewn up… well almost. There's another gang working the racecourses, and between the two outfits they have every bookie from Wolverhampton, Warwick, and Worcester paying them protection money.' Shotgun Charlie paused for another sip.

'So what's this King Arthur's interest in me? Why is he suddenly deciding to muscle in down here? Hasn't he got enough to control up there?' The Spaniard asked.

'Well, that's just it, he does. He already has more than he can handle, especially with this other gang vying for interests on his so-called racecourses. But he has a rather ambitious son, who is trying to build his own reputation away from Daddy's shadow. He's out to prove to his father that he is a worthy successor, and the talk is that he is the one trying to get a foot in the door down here.'

'What's this little fucker's name?' The Spaniard asked.

'Vince. Vince Connelly. He's a vicious little bastard. Got himself a bit of a reputation with a cut-throat razor. He always carries a blade with him and is only too willing to leave its mark on those who cross him. Mind you, he ain't in his father's league. King Arthur has slain more people than syphilis.'

'I didn't know you could die of syphilis,' The Spaniard said.

'You can if you give it to King Arthur,' Charlie chuckled.

'So which one do I go after?' The Spaniard asked, more to himself than to Shotgun Charlie.

'If you go after Vince, then King Arthur will certainly come down on you, and if you take out the old man, then you'll be doing Vince a favour, but I doubt he will thank you for it. My advice would be stay well clear of the whole fucking lot.'

The Spaniard gave Shotgun Charlie a steely stare. 'But I didn't ask your advice, did I, Charlie?'

'No, sorry... no you didn't,' Charlie sheepishly murmured, taking another long glug of his pint.

'Who heads up this rival gang there?' The Spaniard asked.

'That's the Morgan brothers. A couple of sheep-shaggers from over the Welsh border. They're tough, but there's no real brains in the outfit.'

The Spaniard turned away, lost in thought. After a long pause he looked back at Shotgun Charlie. 'That's good. You did well, Charlie. I think I've just thought of a way of resolving this little matter. I need you, Tel-Boy, and Pete the Pig ready on Friday. We're going to give those Brummies a big surprise.'

'Will there be expenses thrown in?' asked Shotgun Charlie.

'Yeah, don't worry. I'll look after you,' The Spaniard replied. 'Here's a pony to be getting along with, and to cover your last trip.' The Spaniard slipped a brown envelope across the table with twenty-five big, crisp, green one-pound notes in it. 'Be at the Club 10am Friday. OK?' With that, The Spaniard got up from the table and walked out of the pub.

2005

'So come on, Sambo, how was she? Did you give her a right good porking?' Pepe asked. A week had passed since Samir's birthday, and unusually for the two of them, they hadn't seen each other during that time. They had both been busy tied up with different jobs during the week. But now they were in their usual greasy spoon, where they went every Saturday morning. The owner of the cafe – a very disagreeable Chinese man named Fuk Yu Tu – would have been very upset to hear it referred to as a greasy spoon. He had given it the somewhat grandiose name of The Jade Palace, and advertised it as English bistro by day, cordon bleu Chinese by night. Unfortunately, he had misspelt the cordon bleu in the window and it read 'English bistro by day, Gordon Blue by night'.

'Hang on, hang on, let me get some cutlery first,' Samir said, getting up and going over to the counter.

'Hurry up then, I wanna hear all about it,' Pepe said excitedly. 'I bet she was a right filthy little minx!'

Samir called across the counter, 'Got any cutlery?'

Two small serving hatch doors opposite him flew open, and a little Chinese head popped through them. 'You know where cutlery. It over there. It always over there. You stupid.'

'Oh, yes,' Samir replied, 'I keep forgetting, over by the window. Sorry... Fuk Yu Tu,' grinned Samir, as he fetched the knives and forks and sat back down at the table with Pepe.

'Tell you what, Dorothy, my nadger ain't half sore. I must have given it to her four bleedin' times. She was all over me like eczema!' Samir gloated.

'Four times! You little stud, no wonder there was so much moaning going on,' Pepe laughed. 'I could hardly concentrate on her brother with all that noise coming through the wall. I thought she had you in a half nelson.'

'Wouldn't mind if she had, be less weird than sticking her finger up my bumhole while I was giving her one,' Samir said, frowning.

Pepe burst out laughing. 'You what? She put her finger up your *Khyber Pass*?'

'Yeah, and gave it a right good wiggle around in there, crazy cow!'

'Nice one! Good girl,' Pepe said, still laughing. 'Nothing wrong with a polite fingering, Sambo, me old mate.'

'It's alright for you, Dotty, you're used to things up your Dartford Tunnel. This took me totally by surprise, I didn't know whether I was coming or going.'

'So what did you do?' asked Pepe.

'Shot me load straightaway. As soon as she gave it a wiggle. Bugger me, it was brilliant!' laughed Samir, slightly embarrassed.

'Ha! So you liked it, then? You'll be wearing heels and picking out fabrics next,' encouraged Pepe.

'Leave it out, it was just a finger, mate. The last thing I want is some boner up me backside.'

'Mmm... that's what they all say to begin with,' mocked Pepe. 'Buggery has such a bad name for itself. Really, it's a bit like drowning – a lot of thrashing around at the beginning, and shortness of breath, but once you relax it really is very pleasurable.'

'Yeah, whatever, bumboy! I know what my arse is for, thank you very much. And that reminds me,' said Samir, as he got up from the table and went towards the toilet, 'there's a Mr Brown waiting in the departure lounge. Be back in a bit.'

'Charming!' called Pepe after him.

'So, are you going to see her again?' Pepe asked when Samir returned from doing his business.

'See who?' Samir asked.

'Bugger me, Sambo. Bianca. We were just talking about her. You've got the retention of a goldfish, you have.'

'Nah, shouldn't think so.'

'Why not?' asked Pepe.

'Gotta spread the love, man, spread the love,' grinned Samir. 'Anyway, I've got a date with Chantelle and Chardonnay tonight.'

'Who the bleedin' heck are Chantelle and Chardonnay?' Pepe inquired.

'You know? Those two birds from Essex. You remember? I was dancing with them in the club before I started chatting up Bianca. The pair of slappers with long black hair and white handbags. I saw them last Tuesday, they stayed over at my place. I gave them a right good portion,' beamed Samir.

'What! Both of them?' Pepe sat back, shaking his head in disbelief. 'In your bed at once?'

'Yezzum,' winked Samir.
'Good grief, Sambo, what a week you've had. You must have been *cream crackered* after all that.'

'Well, to tell you the truth, I did wake up feeling a bit stiff,' winked Samir.

'I bet you did, dear!' scoffed Pepe.

'Anyway, enough about me. You left Bianca's flat pretty early the next morning. How did you get on with the little brother?' Samir asked Pepe.

27

'Not so little, as it turned out.' Now it was Pepe's turn to beam. 'He was a dark horse, that one. I thought he was all young and innocent, turned out he was a right power bottom. Plus, he had a massive todger on him, with a kink in the middle.'

'Alright, alright,' shouted Samir, 'spare me the details, please. Let me breakfast go down.'

'Well, you asked,' defended Pepe. 'You should have seen it. When he got a chubby on, it was so big and bent, he could have popped it round the corner and given you a little treat too!'

'Oh enough, please,' Samir said, raising his hands. 'I'm going to pay the bill.' He went up to the closed serving hatches and shouted, 'Fuk Yu Tu!'

The doors banged open. 'Wha you wan?' called the sweat-covered little Chinese face from within.

'The bill. We wanna pay,' said Samir.

'Eight pound. Me busy. You leave on counter,' came the reply.

'Eight pound? Why's it always eight quid regardless of what we order?' asked Samir. 'Every week the same, always eight quid.'

'Eight vely rucky number for Chinese,' smiled Fuk Yu Tu, revealing an empty mouth with the exception of one very yellow-looking incisor.

'You're a sandwich short of a picnic, you are,' nodded Samir.

'Yeah,' shouted Fuk Yu Tu. 'Me sandwich, but you ugly!' And he slammed the hatch doors closed again.

'Come on, Dorothy, let's get out of this nuthouse,' Samir called to Pepe, slapping down the eight quid on the counter. As they were going out the door, they both turned around, just as they did every Saturday morning, and shouted, 'Fuk Yu Tu!' at the top of their voices, and then ran out giggling like a couple of naughty schoolboys before the serving hatch doors flew open again.

1975

Tel-Boy stopped outside the Club bang on 10am. The Spaniard, Pete the Pig, and Shotgun Charlie were standing outside having a smoke, when the white Range Rover with blacked-out windows pulled up. As they climbed into the spacious cockpit, the newsreader made an announcement on the radio.

'This just confirmed. Two out of the thirteen hostages being held by the Baader-Meinhof in the German embassy in Stockholm have been shot dead by their captors. A spokesman for the Baader-Meinhof, or as he referred to it – The Red Army Faction, confirmed that this act was in retaliation for Chancellor Helmut Schmidt's refusal to negotiate and give in to their demands to release their comrades from Stammheim Prison. They went on to say that they will start killing one hostage every hour, unless negotiations recommence.'

'Fucking Kraut lefties,' spat Shotgun Charlie.

'Morning, chaps,' Tel-Boy cheerily called, turning down the radio.

'Alright, Tel,' Pete the Pig was the only one to respond. The Spaniard got in the back with Shotgun Charlie, and within thirty minutes they were on the M1 heading north towards Birmingham.

The Spaniard was talking over the finer points of his plan with Charlie, while Tel-Boy and Pete the Pig were discussing the merits of bacon butties over sausage sarnies.

'I'm *Hank Marvin*,' said Pete the Pig.

'You're always bloody starvin', you,' said Tel-Boy.

'I can't help it, I have a very high metamorphosis,' whined Pete.

'You what? Metamorphosis? You mean metabolism, you daft twat,' laughed Tel-Boy. 'There's an orange in the glove box if you're that hungry,' he offered.

'Nah, I can't eat fruit,' Pete the Pig grunted.

'Why can't you eat fruit?' Tel-Boy asked.

'It's bad for you,' Pete replied.

'What fuckin' planet are you on?' Tel-Boy turned to Pete, aghast. 'How can fruit possibly be bad for you?'

'Well, it didn't do my Uncle Horace any good. My Auntie Flo used to make him eat a piece of fruit every evening before he went to bed. Then suddenly, when he was seventy-seven he just dropped down dead.'

Tel-Boy couldn't quite believe what he was hearing. 'He lived till he was seventy-seven, Pete, what's that got to do with fruit? He simply died of old age!'

'Aah well, that's where you're wrong, Tel-Boy, coz he died eating a piece of apple. Evidently it got stuck in his windpipe, the poor old bugger choked to death!'

'Will you two spastics shut the fuck up!' interrupted The Spaniard from the back seat. 'Me and Charlie are trying to have a proper conversation back here. It's like having the fucking Waltons in the front. Tel-Boy, concentrate on the road. Pete, here's a bag of bitter lemons. Now hush, the pair of yer.'

2005

'Hey, Dotty, what you up to today?' Samir asked on the phone.

'Mum's back in hospital, she's got another round of chemo to get through.'

'Oh shit. I'm sorry – I forgot it was this week. How is she?' Samir asked Pepe.

'You know her, tough as old boots. She's putting on a brave face, but it's breaking my heart seeing her go through this.'

'I know, mate, I know. Can I come with you to see her?'

'Thanks, Sambo, she would really like that. I'm going up there this afternoon. She's in the Royal Marsden. Come over my gaff around midday, and we'll hop over there together.'

'No worries, see you then.'

Pepe put down the phone a little happier, knowing Samir would come with him to see his mum. After all, she thought of Samir as one of her own. In fact, when Pepe and Samir were younger, Pepe use to get quite jealous of the love and affection his mum poured over Samir. Not that he ever said anything about it, just kept it bottled up inside, like he did about everything else. And how could he complain when he loved Samir too, he was the brother he'd always wanted.

Pepe and his mother had moved next door to Samir when Pepe was just three years old, after his mother had walked out on Pepe's father. It had been one summer's evening when she just decided she'd had enough. She left a shepherd's pie and a rhubarb crumble in the oven, and a note for Pepe's father, then walked out with one full suitcase, her jewellery box, Pepe, and his teddy, Elvis.

The note simply read: *'If you really care about us as much as you say you do, then you will let us go.'*

The first two nights after that were spent at Pepe's Auntie Pru's house. She was his mother's older, and very strict, disapproving sister. Two nights was just long enough before the old sores of a feuding childhood together burst open, and covered both his mother and aunt in bitter quarrelling pus. Then, after pawning all her jewellery, desperate to get a place of her own, Pepe's mother managed to put down a deposit on a small flat near Notting Hill. The old slums of Rachman's era were beginning to be cleared, and the big old original houses that had been chopped up into multiple flats were getting a new lease of life.

The flat opposite them in the same building was occupied by a West Indian family – Samir and his father – Winston Gladstone Baldwin III. Which for a London Underground driver was a very grand name, but most people knew him simply as Winnie.

Everyone loved Winnie. He was a kind, soft-spoken, polite gentleman. It was a real shock to the neighbours when Samir's mother had suddenly decided to run off with the milkman – Gold Top Eric – the previous summer, leaving Winnie and Samir to cope on their own. No one could believe she would want to leave someone like Winnie, despite the fact that Gold Top Eric had quite a reputation. It was well known amongst the street gossipers that he was very well endowed in the trouser department, and often gave the housewives an extra pint. Anyway, most people concluded Winnie was better off without her, even though it left poor Samir without a mother in his life. But all that changed when Pepe and his mum moved in opposite.

Samir was the same age as Pepe and they quickly became inseparable. Winnie had been struggling, trying to hold down a full-time job on the tube and looking after Samir at the same time. So when Pepe and his mum arrived, she soon got stuck in with helping Winnie in any way she could. On weekdays she would take both Pepe and Samir off to school, and collect them in the afternoons, then give them their tea before Winnie got back from work. Very often on a Friday night Winnie would return the favour by cooking a feast of chicken roti and shrimp curry, all washed down with bottles of Jamaican Red Stripe beer. This was the one evening that all four of them looked forward to.

Pepe and Samir grew up together, living opposite each other for the next sixteen years. And with Samir spending most of his time round at Pepe's, he came to regard Pepe's mum almost as his own, just as she did him. Even after Samir and his father moved to North London when he was nineteen, he still spent most of his time back at Pepe's. The two of them had been through everything together. Shared every experience shoulder to shoulder – starting the first day at their junior and secondary schools, having their first fag behind the bike sheds, playing for the local football team, snogging Camilla Barker-Fowlds in the bus stop, seeing the hair suddenly sprout out from their testicles, and their voices drop four octaves during puberty. Having their first wank over Winnie's misplaced *Penthouse* magazine. Failing their 'O' levels together. And being arrested on two separate occasions. Once for minor assault while under the influence of alcohol, and once for sexually lewd behaviour while under the influence of cannabis.

During their twenties they had rented a flat together, but were eventually forced out by the landlord after endless complaints about the noise and all-night parties. By the time they hit thirty, just three years ago, they both had their own places, were earning good money and running their own scaffolding company together. Over the years Samir had been engaged twice, but had broken it off both times just before the big day, due to a very nasty outbreak of cold feet. And Pepe had got through a legion of boyfriends, one-night stands, and blow jobs on Hampstead Heath.

1975

The idea was to put the frighteners on Vince Connelly, and make him believe that it was his rival gang – the Morgans. Hopefully, then a bitter feud would ensue, resulting in a lot of bloodshed, and keep Vince so busy up in the Midlands that his trips to London and encroachment on The Spaniard's turf would be abandoned. If the plan succeeded, then The Spaniard wouldn't have to go into battle against this King Arthur, and Prince Vince might get a right good kicking into the bargain. It almost went off without a hitch, but unfortunately Shotgun Charlie got a bit trigger happy, and some poor sod got in the way.

King Arthur owned two large betting shops in Solihull, which Vince oversaw for him. Just before closing time around 6pm on a Saturday, Vince would visit them both and pick up the week's takings. Being a bookmaker's, all the takings were in cash. During the week there wouldn't be a very large amount, unless there was a big race meet, and then Vince would make an extra trip to collect. But mainly during the week, the managers kept the cash securely in the safe until the weekend. Saturdays were always far more lucrative, both shops full all day with a constant flow of flutterers, eager to gamble away their weekly pay packets. The takings were at least four or five times more than on weekdays, mainly due to the numerous race meetings and football matches scheduled for the day.

The plan was for Pete the Pig and The Spaniard to wait for Vince to turn up at the first betting shop, and at the same time, Tel-Boy and Shotgun Charlie would pay a visit to the second one.

At 5.30pm Vince's flame-red Triumph Spitfire screeched to a halt outside Camelot Bookmakers. He hopped out followed more slowly by his passenger. A huge bloke twice his size, a real ape of a man.

'Nice motor!' Pete the Pig enthused to The Spaniard.

'Looks like a fuckin' hairdresser to me,' The Spaniard replied, focusing on Vince as he swaggered across the road and into the shop.

'OK, you know what to do?' The Spaniard said, nodding at Pete the Pig as they crossed the road behind them and headed for the door. 'You keep the big ape busy, while I have a little word with our faggot friend. Then we grab the loot and out, quick as you please!'

'He's a bit bloody big,' Pete the Pig said warily, eyeing up the ape through the glass of the door as they approached.

'Just crack him hard as you can on the knees with the baseball bat, he'll go down like a sack of shit. Now get that balaclava on, I don't want this coming back on us.'

The Spaniard pushed open the door so hard that it nearly knocked the ape over. Pete the Pig saw his opportunity and brought the baseball bat thundering down on him while he was still reeling from the door. Vince turned and saw The Spaniard coming at him and tried to leap over the counter towards the back of the shop. But he wasn't quick enough. He landed awkwardly half on and half off the counter. The Spaniard grabbed his left leg with both hands and yanked Vince towards him. He came flying back off the counter and smacked face down onto the floor. As he rolled over to look up at his assailant, he received the most almighty kick in the ribs. Just then, a powerful arm roughly grabbed The Spaniard's right shoulder, swinging him round. It was the ape lurching forward at him, with Pete the Pig wrapped round his ankles still trying to bring him down. But The Spaniard was far too quick for this lumbering giant, and caught him hard with a left upper cut to the chin. Then swinging under his grip, and getting behind him, he slammed the ape's head down on the counter, smashing his nose open. The three shop girls behind the counter were screaming, and the remaining four punters had made for the door.

'Get the fuckin' cash!' The Spaniard roared at Pete the Pig, then gave the ape one final giant push, sending him flying backwards onto a table and two chairs, which collapsed under his falling weight. The Spaniard then pulled Vince up by the scruff of his collar. 'Where's your fuckin' blade, you little gobshite?'

'What?' Vince burbled.

The Spaniard felt into the pocket of Vince's tight white jeans and ripped out the cut-throat razor. 'This fuckin' blade!' The Spaniard then grabbed hold of Vince's left ear and sliced part of it off.

'Now your friends can call you Vince fuckin' Van Gogh! This is from the Morgan boys. We don't want you on our fuckin' racecourses any more. You run and tell Daddy that all the course bookies belong to us. He can keep his little empire in the city, but we run the races. Alright!' He then punched Vince hard in the stomach, completely knocking the wind out of him, and dropped him to the floor.

'Sorry, girls,' he nodded at the counter staff, as he took one of the bags of money from Pete the Pig and nonchalantly walked out, giving the ape a last crack in the head with his steel-toe-capped taupe suede boot on the way.

The Spaniard and Pete the Pig then drove across town to pick up Shotgun Charlie and Tel-Boy at the agreed rendezvous.

'Alright, boys,' The Spaniard called over his shoulder as the two of them climbed into the back of the Range Rover.

'Yeah, easy peasy!' Shotgun Charlie sneered. 'Reckon there must be nearly a thousand quid in here,' he said, throwing the duffel bag into The Spaniard's lap. 'We've had a right little earner here, lads,' he added.

'Come on, Piggy, hit the gas, let's get out of this dump.'

The Range Rover thundered out of Solihull on the A34 towards Oxford, and then across to London.

Shotgun Charlie continued in his high spirits. 'Did you see the look on that geezer's face when we bundled in through the door. Couldn't believe his *mince pies*. I reckon he must've shit himself right there on the spot. Then this other old fart starts having a go at me. Unbelievable! Silly old cunt, I shoved him so hard his fuckin' *Irish* fell off. What a laugh, he's on all fours trying to pick up his hair, and old Tel-Boy here steps over him calm as you please and asks the girl for the takings. He was so polite, I thought he was gonna lay a bet on the 6.30 at Epsom,' chuckled Shotgun Charlie. 'How did you two boys get on?' he asked The Spaniard and Pete the Pig.

'We had to deal with King bloody Kong!' declared Pete the Pig. 'Vince's henchman. Honest, you should have seen him, he was a monster! Mind you, he was no match for me. I still managed to bring him down,' boasted Pete the Pig.

The Spaniard gave him a despairing glance but said nothing. Instead he turned to Tel-Boy in the back of the motor. 'You're a bit quiet. Everything OK?'

'Better ask John Wayne here,' Tel-Boy said, nodding at Shotgun Charlie.

'What's that s'pose to mean?' Shotgun Charlie scowled at Tel-Boy. 'You better watch your mouth, my son,' he spat.

'Hey, hey! Calm down,' The Spaniard shouted. 'What's he talking about, Charlie?'

'Fuck knows. Better ask him,' Shotgun Charlie sulked.

'Tel-Boy?' The Spaniard enquired, 'What happened back there? What do you mean John Wayne?'

There was a long pause. Tel-Boy was torn between bad-mouthing Shotgun Charlie or lying to The Spaniard. After a moment's consideration, and realising there really was only one choice, he said, 'You said no shooters, right, boss?'

'Yes, I distinctly said I didn't want guns involved, too many innocent bystanders around.'

Tel-Boy went quiet again. He could feel Shotgun Charlie's psychotic glare burning the side of his face.

The Spaniard turned to Shotgun Charlie. 'Did you take a shooter with you, Charlie?'

'Of course I took a fucking shooter with me.' Now Shotgun Charlie was really losing his temper. 'You said you wanted me to hold up a bloody bookmakers and frighten a few punters. What was I gonna take, a bloody Etch-A-Sketch and draw a scary face?'

'Yes, but you didn't have to use it, did you?' Tel-Boy piped in.

'Oh, fuck me, don't tell me you shot someone?' The Spaniard asked Shotgun Charlie.

'It was just a flesh wound, he's not dead or anything.'

'You shot him in the back,' Tel-Boy said, unable now to hold back.

'What the fuck did you need to shoot someone in the back for?' asked The Spaniard.

'He was running out the shop. He had seen my face,' replied Shotgun Charlie.

'Seen your face? Seen your fucking face? Where the fuck was your balaclava?' The Spaniard asked.

'I didn't put it on, we just went in so quick, I didn't bother with it, alright?' Shotgun Charlie snapped.

The Spaniard turned back and stared out of the windscreen. He momentarily composed himself, before asking Tel-Boy in a more restrained tone, 'How bad was he hurt, Tel?'

'He took a barrel in his lower back. He was still alive on the pavement when we left.'

'Were you wearing your balaclava?' The Spaniard asked Tel-Boy.

'Yes, boss.'

'OK… good lad. Pete, pull off at the next right, under that bridge. Me and Charlie are gonna take a little walk.'

2005

'I need a drink, bro.' Pepe glanced across at Samir. His mother had been very drowsy when they arrived. They had sat with her for thirty minutes, but there was little point in remaining as she was so zonked out. Had Pepe been there on his own, he would have stayed much longer, unable to leave her so soon, sitting holding her hand, waiting for even the smallest flicker of confirmation from her. Some reassurance that she knew he was there by her side, watching over her. But he was very conscious of Samir's presence, and the two of them sat in a depressing fidgety silence. The longer they stayed, the more he sensed Samir might become restless. This was in actual fact untrue. Samir felt nearly as compelled as Pepe to stay with her. Having not visited her in the hospital on the previous occasions, he now felt more distressed than Pepe seeing her today in this condition. An awful feeling of guilt that he hadn't been before bore down on him. In his defence, her previous hospital stays had been fairly brief, and Samir had thought that she was recovering and doing fine. He now sat in silence, not through awkwardness or boredom as Pepe might have thought, but twisted with pain and upset at realising just how ill she really was.

During the thirty minutes sitting with her, she had opened her eyes a couple of times, albeit more a flicker than anything else. And at one point she seemed to nod while Pepe spoke to her. A nurse had come over to check the IV line and monitor. Pepe questioned her about the treatment, part of his determined quest to hear something positive, always hoping to find some renewed glimmer of hope. This was his mother's fourth helping of chemotherapy. She had small-cell lung cancer and was receiving a combination treatment of chemo and radiotherapy. It was knocking the stuffing out of her, indiscriminately destroying both good and bad cells, killing off the healthy with the cancerous, in a savage attempt to stop the spread of this despicable disease. She was now just over halfway through the torturous cycle of treatment, and until it was complete, and new tests carried out, nobody was able to give Pepe the reassurances he was so desperate to hear. He yearned for the day when some hero in a white coat and clipboard would commit to telling him that it was all going to be OK. That it had all been worthwhile, the spread of evil halted and the pain subsiding. But until then, he went through every hospital visit the same, feeling anxious and hopeless, and leaving frustrated and depressed.

1975

'Come on, mate, what yer getting yer knickers in such a twist about? We got a sack full of cash, put the shits up Prince Vince, and got away scot free. That's what you wanted, wasn't it?' Shotgun Charlie argued with The Spaniard as they entered underneath the old railway arches. 'And what the fuck are we doing messing about out here? I'm freezing my nuts off. Can't we get back in the motor?' He whined.

'You shot someone, Charlie. An innocent,' The Spaniard calmly replied, leading the way into the long tunnel.

'It was only a flesh wound, he'll be fine. He was halfway out the door when I popped him, most of the lead hit the door frame.'

The Spaniard now turned to face Shotgun Charlie. 'You were bang out of order, you stupid fuckwit. You just don't get it, do you?' he said menacingly.

'Hey, hang on a minute! Who you calling a fuckwit? I don't have to take this shit from you. Who the fuck do you think you are, anyway, you dago bastard?' Shotgun Charlie was riled now.

The Spaniard gave him an icy stare. 'You've just made us front-page news. The fuzz are going to be all over this, and you've just given them a head start by not covering your ugly mug. I don't need this kind of heat, Charlie.'

'Bollocks!' Shotgun Charlie growled, 'Nobody's gonna finger me. Those punters were shit scared, nobody took a good look at me. What you worrying about, you big girl's blouse?'

'I'm not worried, Charlie. It's you that should be worried. This is where we part company. I don't want to see you or hear from you. You stay well away from me from now on. In fact, it would be better for everyone if you took a long holiday somewhere.'

'Fuck off! I ain't hiding from no one. I can't believe I'm hearing this, I thought you were meant to be some fuckin' hard case. First sign of a bit of trouble and you're wobbling like a jelly, and they call you the fucking Hammer! What a joke.'

The crack of Shotgun Charlie's jaw splintering echoed right through the eight rail arches. Even Tel-Boy and Pete the Pig sitting in the warm comfort of the Range Rover heard it. Shotgun Charlie slumped down on the muddy ground. He was still conscious, but only just. Two of his teeth were broken, and his jaw fractured. His head was spinning, everything was hazy, he felt nauseous. The punch had come from nowhere, with the force of an exocet missile.

The Spaniard stood over him and dropped a wad of notes on the ground next to him. 'I mean it, Charlie, this is the end of the line for you and me.' He then turned and walked back to the waiting car, leaving Shotgun Charlie in swollen agony.

2005

The old man hunched up as he tried to keep warm against the bitter early evening chill. It had been miserably cold and grey all day, and now as he took his first step out of the sheltered housing flat, the sleet started to come down. He turned up the collar of his thick old Crombie overcoat, and pulled his felt trilby hat down lower, trying to block out the ice-cold rain. It was a twenty-minute walk to his local – The Black Jack – a walk that he did every day religiously. Usually it would be lunchtime when he set off, stopping of at the bookies for an hour or so first. He would sit quietly, meticulously studying the form, before picking out four horses. He liked to place multiple bets, where any winnings would roll over onto the next one. His favourite being a yankee, which gave him a total of eleven bets on just four selections. And as long as two or more of the horses came in he was guaranteed a return. He occasionally got lucky and scooped up two or three grand or more, but that was a pretty rare event. His initial stake was usually on the low side, and the odds given on each nag were seldom very inspiring, but it was a harmless way of spending time. It broke up the long and lonely cold days for him, and gave him a bit of an interest. Something to get him out of the depressing four walls, and break up the boredom.

After watching the races, and often as not kissing goodbye to his wager, he would then proceed to the pub for a couple of hours. But today, because of the foul weather and the BBC showing his favourite old movie – *One Flew Over the Cuckoo's Nest* – he had spent the afternoon on the sofa instead, enjoying the manic charm of Jack Nicholson and a youthful Danny

Devito. It was now just after 6pm, and he was itching to get out of the flat. He hated being cooped up all day in that place, and he fancied a couple of pints of pale ale, before picking up a fish and chip supper.

He quickened his pace without noticing the big puddle in front of him – splosh! His left foot landed right in the middle of it. 'Shit!' he muttered as the water seeped in through the slit in his brown leather brogue. Just last week he had been forced to make a cut in the shoe to allow room for his gout-swollen big-toe joint. He had promised to buy himself a pair of those soft comfy-looking hush puppies that everyone in his block seemed to be wearing. He cursed getting old, and all the tedious ailments that went with it. He remembered feeling young and strong, in his prime – muscular and handsome. How he longed for those days now.

1975

'Hello, pet! You're looking very dapper today,' called Peggy as she sprayed the bar with a generous helping of Mr Sheen, not noticing the ash from the permanent fag in the corner of her mouth dropping in her coffee.

'Afternoon, Peg. Is the boss in?' The Spaniard asked, nodding towards Harry's office.

'No, pet, no sign of the idle so and so. Reckoned he was going down the cash and carry. More likely the coach and horses. He was meant to pick me up some bleach to get the basins done. Can't trust the old sod to do even the simplest of tasks.'

'OK. Well, why don't you pop the kettle on while I wait for him?' The Spaniard grinned over at Peggy.

'If I have to, but don't blame me if I don't get all this finished. Honestly, I think I'm the only one that does anything around here.'

Just then Harry walked in.

'Hello, H. How are you?' The Spaniard greeted him.

'What time you call this?' shouted Peggy. 'I hope you got me the bleach.'

'Yes, dear, don't drink it all at once, will you?' Harry plonked the large bleach bottle on the bar.

'Not there, you great lummox! I've just polished that,' yelled Peggy.

'Where shall I put it?' asked Harry, then muttered quietly to himself, 'up your ample arse, dear?'

'Harold Potter! I heard that. I'll give you a right good biffing in a minute.'

'Yes, but not before you've made me a nice cuppa,' interjected The Spaniard. 'Come on, Harry, let's go up to the office, and let poor old Peggy get on with it.'

48

Once up in the office Harry opened the desk drawer and pulled out a copy of the *Daily Mirror*.

'That business up in Birmingham, you said it was all sorted, yeah?' Harry asked The Spaniard.

'Yes… why?' The Spaniard answered cautiously.

'Seen the papers today?' Harry nodded down at the paper on the desk. 'Look at page four.'

The Spaniard picked up the newspaper and started reading.

Camelot comes under siege

A bookmakers in Solihull was the scene of an armed robbery late Saturday afternoon. A neighbouring shop from Camelot Bookmakers called the police after hearing a gunshot and shattering glass.

'Two men, one armed with a shotgun, burst into the shop and demanded the takings,' stated Nancy Postlethwaite – a Camelot staff member.

'We were all petrified,' she added.

During the robbery, a man was shot in the back as he tried to leave the premises. Unconfirmed reports say he was actually a member of the family that own the shop. The premises are reputed to belong to well-known local businessman Mr Arthur Connelly, but as yet no spokesperson for the family has come forward with a statement.

Detective Sergeant Harris from West Midlands Constabulary said they are looking for two men around six feet tall. One was described as big build and masked, the other was slim with red hair, and possibly a cockney accent.

The Spaniard discarded the newspaper onto the desk in disgust.

'How long do you think it will be before old plod catches up with that mug Charlie?' Harry asked him.

'My guess is that King Arthur will find him long before the law does,' answered The Spaniard.

'Don't let that bloody liability drop you in it,' Harry sighed.

'Don't worry, H, Shotgun Charlie may be a lot of things, but he ain't a grass. He's old school, he knows when to keep his trap shut. He won't ever put my name in the frame.'

'Yeah, that's as may be, but then again, who knows what that psycho would come out with, particularly if King Arthur's holding a gun to his head? He's too unpredictable. Disturbed even, the lights are on but no one is home! You never know what you're gonna get next from him. Maybe you should silence him once and for all. Let's face it, you'd be doing a lot of people a favour round here. He's about as popular as a haemorrhoid. Even Myra Hindley has more Christmas cards than him.'

'Harry, Harry please... I never realised you were so fond of him,' chuckled The Spaniard.

'Yeah, well, you know I'm just looking out for you, that's all. You've never let any crap land on you. You're much smarter than any one of those other mugs out there. Don't let your guard down on this one.'

'I know. Thanks, Harry.' The Spaniard put his arm around Harry's shoulders and gave him a squeeze. 'Don't worry, H, it's all under control.' But at the back of his mind, The Spaniard was having doubts himself. The fact that the poor bugger who got an arseful of lead might be one of the Connelly clan could really spell trouble. Hopefully, it would still go as planned, with the Morgan Brothers getting the blame. But if someone did finger Shotgun Charlie for it, then The Spaniard would have a bloody war on his hands.

'Tea's up,' called Peggy as she barged into the office without knocking. She took one look at the two of them with the opened newspaper on the desk.

'Heavens above, is this all you two have to do? Sit round drinking tea and reading the newspaper? It's alright for some,' she tutted. 'You can always come down and give those glasses a once over, filthy they are. I don't know what that young Georgie does at night, idle little sod. I thought he was suppose to be the washer-upper? It's not my job, you know? I reckon he's allergic to water, that one. Come to think about it, he don't half *pen and ink*, plus he looks like he ain't had a bath for a month.'

She was just on her way back out of the door when Harry called, 'Hey, where's my cuppa? You've only brought one mug.'

Peggy turned back and fixed him with a withering look. 'You have got to be kidding me, don't you think I've got enough on my plate without running round after you as well? You want tea, make it yourself.' And she slammed the door closed behind her.

2005

'Evening, Ignacio! Bit late for you today. We was wondering what happened to you.'

'Hello, Wally,' Ignacio greeted the barman, as he placed the trilby on the bar and slipped off his overcoat. 'It's atrocious out there. Didn't fancy going out in it this afternoon. Plus I got too caught up watching *One Flew Over the Cuckoo's Nest* on the box. Terrific film that. You ever seen it?' he asked Wally, who smiled back.

'Yeah. Reminds me of this place – surrounded by a bunch of loonies. Present company excepted, of course,' he quickly interjected, giving Ignacio a careful nod. 'I caught the beginning of it,' he continued, 'but then her indoors made me switch it off coz she had one of her headaches. Next thing I know, she's got me in the kitchen peeling bloody spuds all afternoon, while she's laid on the settee merrily chomping her fat face through my tin of Quality Street. Anyway enough about my woes, I should think you've got a bit of a thirst on by now, haven't you?' he asked Ignacio.

'You bet, Wal.'

'Well, we'll soon fix that for you. A pint of the usual?'

'Smashing. Thanks, Wally.' Ignacio glanced round the pub. It was pretty quiet. There were a couple of old fella's sitting at the bar, and some office-looking types huddled round a table in the corner, plus a couple of lads playing darts, with a third watching them from the sidelines, perched on the bar stool that Ignacio usually occupied. Ignacio clocked him, but went over to the coat rack and hung up his hat and coat first. He then turned and walked across towards the stool.

Wally appeared there first on the other side of the bar with the pint of pale ale. He placed it in front of the lad and said, 'Sorry, kid, but that stool is reserved for yer man here,' nodding in the direction of Ignacio.

The lad looked at Ignacio then back at Wally. 'Yeah! It don't look reserved to me,' he said, taunting Wally.

'Don't be a chump. He's an old regular. Now be a good lad and let the gent sit down.'

The lad stared at Wally then back at Ignacio again. He was about to make another wisecrack, but there was something in Ignacio's eyes that stopped him. He stood up and went over and sat at a table by the window, but he did it slowly, and with as much bluster as he could manage.

'Sorry about that,' Wally said to Ignacio. 'Youth of today, huh?'

But Ignacio didn't bother replying, just plonked himself on the stool and sipped his beer.

The pub was split into two separate bars, the lounge and the snug. Ignacio always sat at the corner end of the snug bar. From there he could see down the length of the bar and into the lounge, which invariably had more customers.

After a couple of pints Ignacio noticed the pub had practically emptied. It had always been more of a lunchtime pub, attracting local workmen with a couple of cheap lunch specials on the blackboard outside, Wally's missus being especially talented in the hotpot department. Trade tended to be much slower in the evenings, with the exception of Friday and Saturday nights, Friday benefiting from the after-office drinkers, and Saturday because of Wally's very entertaining quiz night, when he would don a fez and ask all the questions in the style of Tommy Cooper, with extra silly jokes thrown in along the way.

Ignacio ordered one last half, and went to the toilet. When he returned, the three lads who had been playing darts were now up at the bar, and the same one as before was perched on Ignacio's stool again. Wally was out the back changing the barrel, and both the lounge and snug bars were empty. The Gents' door swung closed behind Ignacio as he stepped out of it, and the three lads looked up at him coming towards them. None of the three made any effort to move. He stopped in front of them, staring from one to the other.

'What's your problem, granddad?' asked the taller one in the middle.

Ignacio scratched his chin, as if thinking about a defensive response, but instead he was considering his next move. He muttered, 'Aw, fuck it,' and then let loose.

The next six seconds were a blur, Ignacio moving so quickly that they didn't know what hit them, quite literally. The taller one felt a crack so hard on his cheek bone that his head flew back, hitting the glass shelf above the bar, and his legs crumpled underneath him. The lad on the left was doubled over, having receiving a thundering blow to the stomach, and the cocky lad on the stool was now sprawled on the floor, after the stool was ripped from underneath him and then shoved into his chest with the force of a Boeing 747 taking off. Hearing the commotion, Wally reappeared gripping an old truncheon, but by then the fracas was over. There wasn't going to be any retaliation, the lads were too stunned, the stuffing well and truly knocked out of them. Once they scrambled back to their feet they made straight for the exit, but the cocky one still had the gall to shout, 'We'll fuckin' have you, granddad, you just wait... We'll be back for you!' as he swung out the door and onto the street.

1975

The Spaniard was downstairs in the bar listening to 'The World at One' on Radio 4. They were interviewing some American bloke named Bill Gates, who had just set up a computer technology company called Microsoft. It was all a bit above The Spaniard's intellectual capacity, but nonetheless he listened intently, intrigued by anything to do with technology, the future, or space travel. It was just six years before that Armstrong and Aldrin had amazed the world by walking on the moon, and two years since the Russians had made it into Mars' orbit. Anything to do with space was a huge hit. Every Saturday at 5.15 in the afternoon, families up and down the country settled around the electric fire with tea and toast in front of the TV, waiting in a mixed state of excitement and trepidation for Tom Baker's *Doctor Who* to begin. Kubrik's *2001 – A Space Odyssey* had captured the imagination of everyone, and avant-garde performers like Bowie were inspirational with songs such as 'Life On Mars 'and 'Starman'. Even old Peggy believed she would be spending her holidays on the moon by the year 2000.

Tel-Boy called down from the office, 'Phone for you, boss.'

'Yeah! I'll be there in a minute,' answered The Spaniard.

'I think it's urgent, boss. It's Ron phoning from Rio.'

'Ron?'

'Yeah! Ron... Ronnie Biggs. He says it's urgent.'

'OK, coming,' The Spaniard said, running up the stairs to the office.

'Hey Ron, you old bugger, how you doing?'

'Hello, mate. Not bad, not bad. Listen, I'll have to make this quick, this call is costing me a fortune.'

'Yeah but, Ron, you've got a fortune,' laughed The Spaniard. '£2.6 million you lifted off that mail train.'

'Yeah, me and fourteen others. Fuck knows where all the money is now,' sighed Biggs.

'What do you mean? Surely you haven't blown it already? You must have some still stashed, don't you?'

'I wish,' replied Biggs. 'It's all gone, mate. The escape from Wandsworth, hiding out in Paris, the plastic surgery. That all cost an arm and a leg. I had to pay off all those thieving intermediaries, nobody wanted to touch me back then, not with all that heat… well, apart from you, mate. I don't know what I would have done without you and Freddie the Fix. If you hadn't sorted that passport and flight over to Sydney for me, gawd knows where I'd be. I'm ever so grateful, mate. I really thought it would all work out for me over there… I mean, it started well enough in Melbourne. I had a good four years there, even got myself some construction work. But then the authorities started sniffing around. The boat to Panama, and getting across to Rio, that used up whatever I had left of my share. That's really why I'm calling, mate. Sorry, I hate to ask, but I'm in a bit of a spot here, and you're the only one I know who can help. I just need a few hundred to tide me over for the next couple of months. Raimunda's still not working since giving birth to Michael. Oh, you should see him, mate, he's a right little beauty. Anyway, as I was saying–

'Hey, Ron,' interrupted The Spaniard, 'it's fine. Of course I will help. What do you need? A grand?'

'Nah, mate, nothing like that. Just a monkey would be fine, cheap livin' over here. Things are a quarter the price of London. And it's only a loan, OK? I'll pay you right back. We've got some great ideas happening here. Since they ran that article last year in the *Daily Express* about me, we've been getting quite a few tourists turning up on our doorstep. We're starting to get T-shirts printed up and all sorts. It's a right old laugh, you'll have to come over and see us one day.'

'I'd love to, Ron. Most exotic place me and Maggie have been is Woolacombe. What are the birds like over there?'

'Oh, mate, unbelievable! They're all wearing these skimpy little bikinis, with bodies to die for. Listen, mate, I'm a walking hard-on, my blood pressure must be through the roof. But I've got a good'un in Raimunda. She's a real angel, and little Michael... well they're both adorable. I'm very happy, mate.'

'Good, glad to hear it, Ron. Listen, give me the bank details, and I'll get the money wired over to you as soon as I can.'

The Spaniard came off the phone, turning to Harry and Tel-Boy, who were both looking somewhat quizzical.

'What was all that about?'

'Poor old Ron, needs a few quid to tide him over.'

'Bugger me! You lending money to the great train robbers now? No wonder they say crime don't pay,' chuckled Harry.

'Yeah! But sex does,' replied The Spaniard. 'So I need you and Tel-Boy to get those clit climaxers and Bobby butt-plugs off the desk and round to Pinky's el pronto!'

2005

The big day had arrived, Arsenal versus Manchester United for the FA Cup at the Millennium Stadium Cardiff. Samir was so excited at managing to get hold of two tickets that he was in danger of a bit of wee escaping at any moment. The only problem was that Pepe was an ardent Manchester United fan and Samir a beloved Gunners fan. It was probably the one and only thing that they argued about. That and the virtues of minge versus cock.

They left Paddington station at 9.30am to arrive in Cardiff before noon, in time for a few pints before kick-off. The train was packed and the buffet car heaving. Samir had strongly urged Pepe not to wear his United scarf on a train packed with Londoners going to support Arsenal, but it fell on defiant ears. As it turned out, it didn't make much odds, because the train had its fair share of Man U. fans on it too. As Pepe constantly liked to remind Samir, 'They reckon there are 320 million United fans worldwide, so you're never alone.'

And as Samir would remind Pepe, '90 percent of them don't even know where Manchester is, but they all know where London is – home to the Arsenal.'

There was lots of banter and beer swilling for the two hours on the train, closely followed by another two hours of the same in the pub before the match.

Unfortunately the actual game didn't live up to the hype and was a bit of a disappointment. Both teams had individually made seventeen cup final appearances before, Manchester United with the slightly better record of eleven wins against their various opponents to Arsenal's nine. But on the one and only previous occasion when they had actually met each other back in 1979, Arsenal had been victorious with a 3–2 win.

The stats promised a thrilling contest, but it wasn't to be. Not even the superb skills of Ronaldo, Bergkamp, Rooney, van Nistelrooy, and Ferdinand could ignite the afternoon. After a goalless ninety minutes plus injury time, on a cloudy grey day, the 71,000 spectators were in sombre mood. It was the first FA Cup Final to go to penalties, with Scholes missing the only one, giving Arsenal victory again.

'What a tragic afternoon!' Pepe said to a rather smug-looking Samir.

'Yeah, you're right, nothing worth getting too excited about… I mean it's only the second time that we've taken the Cup from you now,' laughed Samir.

'Oh, come on, Sambo, you can hardly call that a result. One poxy penalty, and even my Aunt Flossy could have knocked that in!'

'You ain't got an Aunt Flossy,' replied Samir.

'Don't be a smart arse, Sambo. Anyway, I don't know why you support them, bunch of Johnny foreigners, one English player out of the lot of them, even the crinkly old manager is a frog.'

'Oh dear, Miss Dorothy is in a tizz. Clearly she needs a sherry to settle her nerves,' teased Samir.
'Yeah, but not here, let's get back to London. We can have a drink on the train,' sulked Pepe.

Samir was by far the more mild-mannered of the two of them, always ready with an amusing quip or jibe to defrost a situation. Pepe's nature was much more intense; a brooder, as his mum called him. He could be stubborn and pushy and sometimes confrontational. He was tough, super competitive and a terrible loser, unlike the calm temperament of Samir, who always chose the path of least resistance, a far more happy-go-lucky character. It was probably this diversity that made them successful business partners, they complemented each other well. Samir was good at chatting up the clients, getting the work in, and being the business front-man, whereas Pepe was good lurking in the shadows, getting the bad payers to stump up, keeping the site running and the lads in step and on time.

The first train back to London was a stopper, and then they had to change at Bristol Temple Meads. While they were waiting in Bristol for the connection, a platform announcement informed them of a forty-five minute wait due to a delay, so they decided to cross over the road and have a quick pint in the pub nearby while they waited. By the time they were in the bar supping a pint, Pepe was in much better spirits, and they were having a laugh about some lad that worked for them called Barry Balls. Because Barry was barely the size of an oompa loompa – measuring just 5 foot 2 inches – Pepe and Samir had nicknamed him 'Tiny Balls'.

Suddenly, halfway through their conversation they were interrupted by a big ugly skinhead drinking with a group of mates at the bar right next to them. He turned to them accusingly. 'Are you talking to me?'

'You what?' said Pepe, slightly taken aback.

'What did you just call me?' said the skinhead, glowering at the two of them.

'Nothing, we were just talking about a mate of ours... Tiny Balls,' smiled Samir.

'There you go again, you calling me tiny balls?'

Now a couple of his skinhead mates turned round and started giving Pepe and Samir the eyeball.

'Leave it out. Listen, how would we know if you have tiny balls?' Pepe asked, not in the slightest bit intimidated by the moron in front of him.

'What are you? Keep talking about balls, some kind of shirt-lifter or something?' the skinhead sneered with contempt.

'Yeah, I am, as it goes,' answered Pepe aggressively. 'But don't worry, you're safe. That whole big boots and diamond knitwear look doesn't do it for me.'

The skinhead looked down at his Pringle sweater flabbergasted, shaking his head in disbelief. 'You what?'

It was then that Pepe noticed the skinhead's clenched fists on the bar. He saw that four fingers on each hand were tattooed with the words 'Love' and 'Hate'. Unfortunately, the skinhead had lost the little finger on his left hand in a work accident, so now his knuckles read 'Love' and 'Hat'.

'By the way,' continued Pepe, now switching into a camp lisp, 'Love the hat!'

The skinhead stared down at his hands, then back up at Pepe, shaking in rage. He grabbed hold of Pepe's United scarf. 'Why you little fucking que–'

But before the skinhead could finish his sentence Pepe, who had been readying himself for this, head-butted him full in the face, and he and Samir were now halfway to the door. One of the other skinheads managed to just grab the back of Samir's hood as he was leaving, but couldn't keep grip after a very panicked Samir swung round and kicked him right in the goolies. Once out on the busy street, they were lucky with a break in the traffic, and managed to negotiate the hectic road and sprint into the train station, where they could easily lose themselves amongst the crowded fifteen platforms.

'Chuffin' Nora! You're bleedin bonkers!' blasted Samir, as they headed for the end of their platform, just as their train was approaching.

'Did you actually clock how many of them there were drinking in there? The place was full of skins.'

'I know, but what a crack, eh?' grinned Pepe as they jumped on the train.

'If that's your idea of fun, you need to find a new playmate. I'll be amazed if my undies aren't soiled, thank you very much. I'm sweating like an eight-year-old backstage in Gary Glitter's dressing room!' Samir said shakily. They were sitting opposite each other in the train carriage, urging it to pull out, both of them nervously staring out of the window, looking across the station to see if they had been followed by the skinheads. Then, just as the train started up and lurched forward, leaving the platform, they spotted four skinheads jumping over the barrier, trying to catch the rear of their train. The train gathered speed, the doors were securely closed. They looked at each other, both extremely relieved. Then a broad grin appeared on Samir's face, 'Ooh, love the hat, dear!' And they both dissolved into fits of laughter.

1975

The Spaniard and Maggie got out of the black cab at the bottom of the street. They were dressed for the evening, The Spaniard in black tie and dinner jacket, while Maggie looked stunning in a very low-cut white dress, embroidered with tiny turquoise, pink, yellow, and red flowers. It was probably not the appropriate gown for the occasion, but anyone seeing her in it would have little choice but to melt in her beauty. Her twinkling Persian green eyes, and long, wavy, golden-blonde hair could make time stand still.

The atmosphere between the two of them was ice cool. The Spaniard asked the driver to drop them off early to give him a chance to clear the air with Maggie before arriving at the party. They strolled in silence through the impressive leafy square, taking in all the surrounding wealth. On both sides of the square were magnificent white Georgian properties, two of which had blue plaques denoting them as previous residences of a former prime minister and a world-renowned composer. This was the sort of street he had in mind for him and Maggie, right plumb in the middle of Mayfair W1. And why not? He worked bloody hard building his little empire, keeping everybody happy – the filth, the punters – making an example of those who stood in his way. A few more years at this rate, and he would be sitting pretty on a right little pile. He already had the foundations in place, the right premises in and around Soho, the muscle, the right contacts, on both sides of the law. He had come a long way from his humble beginnings back in Deptford with his old dad.

When the old man died a few years back, The Spaniard had finally moved out of the family two-up two-down in Deptford. His mum had passed away from tuberculosis many, many years earlier, when he was just eight years old. It had been hard growing up without a mother's love. His father had tried his best, but he was a tough man, unable to share his feelings and provide the emotional support a child deserves. The Spaniard never doubted his father loved him, but no affection was ever shown or given between them. Fortunately, The Spaniard accepted this at an early age, and it never prevented him from still adoring his father. This was the reason that kept him there till the end in the same house, looking after his father during his final years. After the death, it was time for him to make a fresh start. He wanted something pretty swanky for Maggie, but couldn't afford the high prices of Chelsea and Knightsbridge. Earls Court seemed a good stepping stone. To the east was the Kings Road and Sloane Square, to the north, South Kensington. They rented a very large three-bedroom maisonette on the first and second floor of an old Victorian house. The flat came with a small back patio and a balcony at the front overlooking the enclosed central gardens. But this wasn't enough for him any more, now he wanted something far grander. He was convinced that things would be much better between Maggie and him once he had achieved the next step. And it wouldn't be that much longer if tonight was any indication.

He had received an invitation to Lord Fitzpatrick's private birthday party. It wasn't just the prestige of mixing with the la-di-das, but something far more important that made this a triumphant occasion for The Spaniard. It was through parties like this that he could make even more powerful and influential contacts. Very often those with wealth and status had secrets, naughty habits, or appetites for things that were best kept out of the public domain. The Spaniard was gaining a reputation as a facilitator, a person who could feed those desires with the utmost discretion. This was how he first came under the cloak of Lord Fitzpatrick. It turned out that His Lordship, or Dirty Bertie as he was known by his closest friends, was rather partial to young girls, ideally between thirteen and fifteen years of age, with a bit of colour, and from far humbler backgrounds than M'Lord. The more exotic the better!

One night, after a late drinking session ending in Club Bohemia, Dirty Bertie was feeling a little frisky and within an hour The Spaniard had a dusky fourteen-year-old called Malika sitting on Bertie's lap. M'Lord was terribly impressed and most grateful to his congenial host. Since then, he had become a regular punter at the Club. What M'Lord didn't know was that the fourteen-year-old Malika was actually called Maureen from Tottenham, and had just celebrated her eighteenth birthday. She worked in one of The Spaniard's sex joints on Brewer Street. She was very young looking and willing to do most things for a little extra in her pay packet. She had become quite a talent at role-playing during her brief career working in Pussylicious and knew exactly how to satisfy even the most bizarre requests and fetishes. His Lordship had swallowed it hook line and sinker; he had no idea that the little girl sitting on his lap asking for ice cream had actually just had an abortion and was about to take her driving test for the third time.

Tonight was a big night for The Spaniard, and he needed it to go off without a hitch, to make the right impression, and that meant keeping Maggie sweet.

They were now nearing Lord Fitzpatrick's home, and he was still stumbling over the right words in his head, trying to pitch it right. He knew Maggie was pissed off with him, but what he didn't realise was just how deep her resentment towards him was becoming. She was tired of his irregular comings and goings. She never knew when he would be home, where he was when he wasn't at home, what he was up to, or who he might be up to it with. Not that she wanted to keep tabs on him — she was not the sort to get possessive or jealous. She just wanted a normal existence. She craved some routine. She wanted a reliable man, who she could cook a nice meal for when he came home from work, someone who would spend time with her at weekends. Someone who would talk to her, really talk, and share things, not just demands or expectations.

It had been so different when they first met six years ago, back when she was just nineteen and he was twenty-nine. She had loved the late-night parties with him, out dancing together all night to the Beatles and the Stones. Weekdays in the Soho coffee shops gossiping with the girls, then meeting him later and shopping in Carnaby Street. Saturday afternoons spent cruising up and down the Kings Road with the roof down in his E-Type Jag. Then sunbathing in Hyde Park on Sundays. Back then, they laughed, they talked, they made love with a real hunger for each other. It was the happiest she had ever felt.

As his business interests grew, they started to creep apart, the distance between them opening up. Less and less he wanted her by his side. At first, she understood and accepted this. He was working hard and still made an effort to spend time with her, and bought her whatever she desired. But over the last year or so he had hardly spent any time at home, and the only time he ever took her out was when he needed a bimbo on his arm like tonight. Maggie just wasn't that kind of girl. It was all very nice having money thrown at her to buy dresses and jewellery, but she wasn't willing to accept them as a trade-off to keep her as the happy little trophy wife left at home, only wheeled out when absolutely necessary. She wanted a proper husband and father for her baby.

She felt his arm go round her shoulders and that big strong hand squeeze her tightly.

'Listen, princess, you know I love you, and I'm sorry I haven't been home very much over the last few days.'

Maggie had to bite her tongue. Last few days? More like months.

'But I've been putting in the hours at the Club and building the business up for us. I just want the best for you, and sometimes that means I can't be around as much as I would like to be. But we are together tonight, and look where we are, my princess, mixing with the gentry, knocking back champagne with England's finest. Not bad, eh? You know I take care of you. Let's enjoy tonight together. By the end of it you'll probably be best friends with some countess or whatever.'

Maggie looked up into those big beautiful, coffee-brown eyes. In a way, she felt sorry for him. This broad, rugged, handsome, ambitious man was actually a socially inept little boy inside, trying desperately to impress the very people whose world he would never be accepted into. He thought he was charming them, but they were just using him for their own ends, and would drop him like a hot brick as soon as he outlived his usefulness.

She couldn't be bothered to argue any more, she was tired of fighting. She would concede tonight, but this would be the last time. She went on tiptoes and kissed him on the cheek. Then seeing the mark left by the baby-pink lipstick, she smudged it with the thumb of her white glove, like a mother to a child before he went through the school gate on his first day.

'My dear chap, so pleased you could make it. And who is this divine goddess?' fawned Lord Fitzpatrick.

The Spaniard introduced Maggie to M'Lord.

'Oh, do call me Bertie,' he drooled.

'Now, let me see, who might you know here?' M'Lord said, surveying the room. And what a room it was. Not just the size and grandeur of it, but the haute couture, clipped Etonian accents, diamonds and pearls, titles and upper echelons of society that were contained within it.

'Do you know Lady Wellington?' he asked Maggie, knowing full well that she wouldn't, and in all probability wouldn't know any ladies at all, apart from ladies of the night. However, he thought it his polite duty as host to assume that Maggie and her thug escort – albeit a useful thug – mixed in the same social circles as the rest of his guests.

'Um… no, I don't think so,' replied Maggie, a little overawed by her surroundings. Just then she caught sight of an elegant figure resembling one of the royal family stepping out of the French doors onto the back lawn.

'Is that who I think it is?' she asked M'Lord.

He glanced over to where Maggie was looking. 'Oh, yes, yes, it' Margie. Always good to have around, give the party a bit of sparkle. Let's hope we've got enough gin in! Speaking of which, do have a glass of fizz,' he offered, as a waiter with a tray of champagne flutes sidled up to them.

They chatted for a further ten minutes, just small talk about Club Bohemia and also a new French restaurant in Knightsbridge that was all the rage. By the time M'Lord had finished waxing lyrical about his recent meal there of tortured goose liver, the legs off a frog, some snails, and then a rabbit, Maggie felt positively nauseous. In fact, she was quite relieved when he excused himself to welcome more guests. Before doing so, he asked The Spaniard to join him sometime later for a quiet word in his study before the party ended. 'Nothing too serious, just a little bit of business that I thought you might be able to help with me with,' winked M'Lord.

Maggie watched him glide off to his next batch of guests. 'Goodness gracious, the way he was going on, I thought he was going to tell us they lightly poached the chef and served him up too. I hope you're not thinking of taking me to that froggy restaurant,' Maggie said to The Spaniard.

'No, princess, don't worry. Over-priced rubbish. But all that talk of grub has made me hungry. Let's find where all the nosh is, I've just seen some clown with a tray full of cheese lumps and shit.'

In the taxi on the way home Maggie was full of it. She had actually enjoyed the party far more than she ever thought she would. Not just because she got introduced to a member of the royal family, but they had actually shared a Sobranie cigarette together. In fact, she was so overcome with the excitement of it all she fished the butt end out of the ashtray when no one was looking and kept it as a little memento. After all, not everyone had a filter tip covered in the deep rouge lipstick of a real-life princess.

'What did Dirty Bertie want to see you about in his study?' she asked The Spaniard, half expecting him to give her some cock and bull story. He rarely discussed any of his business activities with her, unless of course he needed her to play some role in it. That suited her just fine. She was wise enough to know that he operated on both sides of the law, and it was better if she was kept in the dark when it came to his more illicit dealings, particularly if violence was involved. She hated that side of it, and though he constantly tried to reassure her that he wasn't mixed up in anything where people got hurt, she knew him far better than that. It actually took her by surprise this time when he answered her question for once, instead of changing the subject as usual. Maybe he had drunk a little too much of M'Lord's 1959 Saint Emilion Grand Cru.

'He just wanted me to meet some friend of his.'

'Really… who?' Maggie asked, suddenly curious about Dirty Bertie and his various friends, particularly after tonight's little soirée.

'What do you mean who?' The Spaniard gave Maggie an inquisitive look. 'Since when were you interested in the affairs of Lord Fitzpatrick?'

'Well, that depends on the affair,' she laughed.

'Well the only affair Dirty Bertie is having is with a fifteen-year-old Ghanaian girl, the last I heard. And as for his friend in the study, I think he's batting for the other side.'

'You what?' Maggie asked.

'You know… he's *ginger beer*, a *baked bean*.'

'Oh,' she giggled. 'So is that why he's interested in meeting a big strong handsome boy like you?' she teased.

'Hey, cut that out,' The Spaniard said sharply, then immediately softening. 'You know I'm a real man,' he grinned, sliding his hand under her dress and up her inside thigh.

'Really? So what do you do all day with Pete the Pig, then?' She winked.

'Now, you know me and Piglet have something special between us.' The Spaniard winked back, enjoying the game, as his two fingers slipped delicately under the lining of her panties. She opened her legs slightly to give his fingers more freedom to reach their soft, inviting target.

'Mmm, well maybe you should leave Mr Piggy alone, and concentrate more on Miss Beaver instead,' she purred.

'Well, maybe I just might,' he replied, deliciously dipping his fingers in her hot moist pussy. 'But only if Mr Cockerel can play too?' he whispered, gently biting her earlobe.

'That'll be a quid, mate!'

The Spaniard jumped up startled. 'You what?'

'I said, that'll be a quid,' called the cab driver over his shoulder. Maggie and The Spaniard burst out in embarrassed laughter, as they realised the taxi had reached their destination and pulled over outside their home.

2005

'Come on, Sambo, let's go down to Brighton Gay Pride, it'll be a right crack.'

'Ah, I'm not sure. I was thinking of going into town and getting some new Shimano gears for my pushbike.'

'You what?' Pepe shouted. 'Flamin' Nora, Sambo! Don't be so bleedin' straight.'

'Well, actually, I hate to disappoint you, Dorothy, but I am bleedin' straight, and proud of it, thank you very much.'

'Yeah, right! Face it, all you straights are really just secret closet cases. Given half a chance most of you would love it up the Chorley Woods.'

'Don't be so puerile,' Samir chided.

'So anyway, what about Pride then?' asked Pepe, changing back the subject. 'You up for it? You loved it last year,' he encouraged.

'Did I?' Samir asked.

'Come on, you know you did. And talk about closet cases. Don't you remember getting all amorous with those two trannies in the Wild Fruit tent? You were giving them a right good grope as I recall.'

'I was not groping them,' Samir spat in disgust. 'I was confused. How was I to know they were cocks in frocks? I'd drunk eight cans and dropped a tab of speed, for goodness sake.'

'Yeah, whatever, dear!' Pepe teased. 'Come on, we can get a train around midday, and be off our tits in the Popstarz tent by 3pm.'

'Well, now that you come to mention it, I guess I don't need new gears that badly,' laughed Samir. 'Meet you at the station.'

The train was a sea of pink and rainbow. It seemed that everyone on it was on their way to Pride. There were more feather boas, glittering sequins, and bottles of vodka than you could shake a big stick at.

Pepe and Samir sat next to two very chatty and cute-looking lesbians, who were both dressed like a couple of tom-boys, in dungarees, with choirboy haircuts, who introduced themselves as Sky and Cheyenne.

'How come lezzers never have normal names?' asked Samir

'Why? What are your names, then?' asked Sky.

'Dorothy and Samantha,' answered Pepe, with a deadpan face.

'Actually, it's Dorothy and Samir,' corrected Samir in the most rugged straight voice he could muster.

'Why? You not a fairy then?' Cheyenne asked Samir, laughing.

But before he could answer, he was interrupted by Pepe again, 'Her? Gay? In that shirt? Of course she is.'

'Hey? What's the matter with this shirt?' asked Samir defensively.

'Honey, tangerine is really not your colour!' lisped Pepe.

'Tangerine? It's not tangerine,' denied Samir, in disgust.

'Well, what is it then? argued Pepe.
'I don't know... maybe... burnt ochre?' Samir suggested sheepishly.

'Burnt ochre? Oh, you're gay alright,' laughed Sky, winking in collusion with Pepe.

By the time they got to Brighton they had missed the parade along the seafront, and most of the floats and scantily dressed participants were heading up towards Preston Park ready for an afternoon of hedonistic pleasure. Samir and Pepe fell in with the crowds of people slowly making their way up the Steine past the Pavilion. On one side of them was a group of six very butch-looking fella's dressed as nuns swigging back Newcastle Brown Ale. They repeatedly lifted their habits, and any unsuspecting passers-by coming in the other direction were greeted by an array of genitalia, ranging from hairy to shaven and pierced to protruding. On the other side were two slim attractive-looking lads wearing tight-fitting white sailor uniforms, with their not so attractive, slightly larger-looking friend who was dressed as a gimp, complete with collar and leash. It wasn't long before Pepe had struck up a conversation with the two sailor boys, and Samir was on his mobile trying to get through to some of their mates who were already down in Brighton for the weekend.

The park grounds were quickly filling up. Pepe and Samir bought a couple of beers from one of the bar tents and wandered over to the market area. They weaved their way through all the stalls, taking in the amazingly diverse products and promotions available. At one stall you could chat to the Samaritans, while the one next door was selling fourteen-inch black dildos. Pepe thought that very handy, considering that if you bought a fourteen-inch black dildo you should probably be speaking to a Samaritan anyway, or at the very least a surgeon. Samir had over-eagerly accepted a leaflet being handed out entitled SLUTS, but was rather disappointed when he saw that it stood for Sussex Lesbian Undertakers Society. And to compound his frustration, he was now being cornered by a very overweight, rather morose, butch-looking dyke, informing him of the joys of a lesbian burial. Pepe could see that Samir was struggling to get away from this calorie consuming carpet-muncher, his sense of political correctness not allowing him to appear uninterested or impolite to a lesbian on this, their day of celebration. Unlike Pepe, who bowled over to Samir and cheerily nodded, 'Who's your friend, dear?'

The undertaker gave Pepe a cursory nod and introduced herself. 'My name is Fatima.'

'Oh, alright. Hi there, Fatty,' Pepe smiled.

'No, I said my name was Fatima. No one calls me Fatty. My friends call me Fatima or just Fat.'

Pepe and Samir glanced at each other.

'I bet they do,' Pepe said out the corner of his mouth. And before Fatima could respond, Pepe concluded with, 'Well, thanks very much, Fatty. If ever we come across a clit-licker that needs cremating we'll give you a shout.' He then linked his arm through Samir's and pulled him away in the direction of the free condoms and lube stall.

After stuffing their pockets with gratis condoms, they bought another four cans of Bud and plonked themselves down on the grass outside the cabaret tent. The park was packed now, and Pepe and Samir sat back soaking up the glorious afternoon sunshine, watching the crowds of people wandering by.

'Where do you think Marco and the other boys have got to?' Samir asked Pepe, referring to their mates.

'Dunno. Have you tried calling them again?'

'Nah, too many people, the signal keeps fading. I sent Blue a text, hopefully, he'll reply.'

'They could be up on druggie hill,' Pepe suggested. 'We could wander up there after these beers and see if we can spot them.'

'Cool, good idea,' replied Samir.

By 5pm the whole place was heaving, the beer tents filled to capacity, the dance tents awash with topless sweating gyrating bodies. The fairground was overrun with thrill seekers, and the numerous food stalls were doing a roaring trade from tofu and couscous to kebab and chips. Pepe and Samir had now met up with some of their mates, and were in the churchyard next to the park indulging in a couple of fat spliffs. One of their friends, Blue, had managed to procure some extremely mind-bending marijuana, fresh from the ancient rolling hills of the North Philippines.

Even the vicar, who momentarily popped out of the church, seemed overcome by the intense sweet aroma that wafted around the gravestones. 'Afternoon, lads,' he cheerfully greeted them.

Ooh, what an exquisite item,' he said, admiring Marco's diamanté-encrusted white-and-gold D&G manbag.

'Cheers, your holiness,' thanked Marco, who was just two puffs away from being totally stoned. '£9.99 from Walthamstow market,' he said to the vicar. 'You wanna get yourself down there, your reverence,' he continued, much to the merriment of Samir and the others.

'I just might do that,' smiled the vicar. 'Does it come in yellow?' he inquired, but was then interrupted by another group, also indulging in a spot of whacky baccy in the graveyard.

They were shouting 'Police!' to warn everyone else as they legged it around the other side of the church, feverishly stubbing out and disposing of their half-smoked joints. Samir and the others did likewise, but instead of running, Pepe coolly led his followers past the two policemen who had just appeared at the gate between the park and the church.

'Afternoon, officers,' he called, as he and his five merry men gleefully trundled past, with Marco grinning inanely back at the officers and shouting, 'Ooh, are you the fashion police? If so, arrest that man.' Pointing at Samir in his tangerine shirt.

Back in the park, the first marquee they stumbled into was the line dancing tent. And without much encouragement, and with even less coordination, all six of them were on the dancefloor making complete prats of themselves, particularly Marco, who fell over twice and was now trying to keep himself balanced by grabbing hold of a very large nipple ring belonging to a big hairy bloke next to him.

'Ooh, you're a big boy, aren't you?' Marco winked up at the leather-clad bear. 'You like jewellery, then?' Marco asked, feeling very giddy, gripping the nipple ring again.

'Yes,' nodded the bear.

'And nice boys like me too?' puckered Marco.

'Yeah, you look kinda cute,' chuckled the bear.

'Hey, girls! I think I just found me a husband,' Marco gleefully shouted to Pepe and the others.

After twenty minutes of frolicking around in the line dancing tent, making complete nuisances of themselves, the group – more tired from laughing, than actual physical exertion – reconvened at the bar in the Revenge tent. By now, the six had become seven, with the inclusion of the nipple-pierced bear, who had taken quite a shine to young Marco, and vice versa. His name was Gary or Stuart or something, but no one cared and they all just referred to him as Daddy Bear. Another two hours of drinking, dancing, chatting and laughing passed, and the group had now swelled in number to a very raucous eleven, Pepe having bumped into the two sailor boys from earlier, and Blue had become rather attached to a Thai language student aptly named Kok.

A guy dressed as a construction worker, who was camper than a fruit salad, was trying desperately to chat up Samir. Samir politely kept trying to tell him that he was straight, and therefore not interested, but the construction worker wouldn't give up. He was now insisting Samir should rub his wallet.

'Go on, honey, just a little rub. It's made of genuine foreskin. The more you rub it, the bigger it will get,' he squealed with delight.

By now Samir's patience had been pushed to the absolute limit. 'Just fuck off, you perv, or I'll shove that wallet right up your jacksy!'

'Ooh, get her!' shrieked the construction worker. 'Don't mind if you do, dearie!'

Samir managed to get Pepe's attention, 'I'm going mad in here. Come on, let's find a toilet, I need to strain my spuds.'

They came across thirty portaloos in a neat row, but the queues were bladder-bustingly long. They decided there was little option but to wait in line. Up ahead they could see Marco and Daddy Bear at the front of one of the queues. One of the loos became free, and Marco and Daddy jumped in together, obviously deciding to share.

After some time, Pepe and Samir noticed that Marco and Daddy had still not emerged from their portaloo, and the loo was in actual fact rocking gently backwards and forwards between the two on either side. The closer Pepe and Samir got as their queue receded, the stronger the rocking motion of Marco's portaloo became. It was pretty obvious, to the delight of the crowd outside, that inside Marco had got rather carried away and was enjoying a damn good rogering from Daddy Bear. Unfortunately Daddy's final thrust was a little too passionate, and as the crowd listening outside applauded his euphoric cry of orgasm, the portaloo rocked so far back and forward that it reached the point of no return. It seemed to remain precariously suspended momentarily at a forty-five degree angle from the ground. There was a loud gasp as the crowd stopped clapping and held its breath. Then the inevitable happened, and the portaloo came crashing door-face down onto the ground.

There was loud yelp from inside, and a lot of cursing, followed by a small plea, 'Please can someone help? Can someone lift us back up?'

The majority of the crowd fell into fits of laughter as a few decent onlookers rushed forward and lifted the portaloo back into its rightful standing position. The grass in front, where the loo had landed, and the cracks of the door were awash with a mix of thick blue toilet disinfectant and urine. You could only imagine what a state it would be inside, a whole afternoon's waste sloshing up out of the trap all over the two of them. It was no surprise that Marco and Daddy waited a full twenty minutes before exiting, concealing their embarrassment until the immediate crowd got bored of waiting to see who, or what, would exit the mini hell, and had dispersed. Those queuing spectators who remained, including Pepe and Samir were treated to a true spectacle when the loo door finally opened, and out stepped Marco and Daddy resembling two putrid-smelling smurfs.

Pepe's group left the park soon after that, and spent the evening in Legends bar down on the seafront getting even more squiffy. By the time they hit Revenge Club they were all totally in the land of 'fuck it!' Marco - having hosed himself down - ended up falling asleep sitting on Daddy Bear's lap, in the corner of the club. Pepe sucked off the two sailor boys in the toilets, while Blue and Kok did a line of coke in the cubicle next door. Leaving Samir and the others in a blissful haze on the dancefloor, popping along to Audio Bullies' 'I shot you down'. Come 5.30am, they were all collapsed on the pebbled beach by the pier, stuffing their faces with greasy burgers, listening to the waves crashing at their feet and watching the sun come up.

1975

The Spaniard, Tel-Boy, and Pete the Pig were all sitting up in Harry's office. The Mike Yarwood Show had just finished, and now they were settling down to watch the big fight on the old Rumbelows black-and-white set. It had been billed 'The Thrilla in Manila,' and Ali had been taunting Frazier at every opportunity: 'It's gonna be a chilla, and a killa, and a thriller, when I get the Gorilla in Manila.'

Harry Carpenter, the sports commentator, was building up the excitement: 'It's the climax to a bitter rivalry between Muhammad Ali and Joe Frazier. Their third fight to settle who is the legitimate heavyweight champion of the world, Ali having been stripped of the title for refusing the draft during the Vietnam war. He had his first professional defeat to Frazier in '71, but won it back in '74. This is it, the final showdown. Ali looking confident after Frazier's recent devastating defeat in round two against a powerful George Foreman, an opponent Ali knocked out in the eighth round in The Rumble in the Jungle, held in Zaire.'

Now it was 'The Thrilla in Manila,' courtesy of Don King and The Philippines President, Ferdinand Marcos, who was desperately seeking good publicity to cover up the social unrest in his country. An uprising against political repression, authoritarian corruption, and human rights violations had resulted in Marcos implementing martial law, but internationally he remained a popular statesman, and this extravaganza would fuel that reputation.

The phone rang in the office. Tel-Boy answered and spoke to Mouse, so called because he always had his ears close to the ground and if he heard any rumours or gossip he would be sure to squeak! He was not The Spaniard's favourite type of person, narks were definitely not tolerated, but Mouse was useful because he proved to be a reliable source of information, and was therefore worth keeping on side for a couple of quid a month.

Tel-Boy came off the phone. 'There's good news and bad news, boss. According to Mouse, Gareth, the older of the Morgan brothers, is in a coma in hospital. Evidently, he got a right good seeing-to. It looks like Vince must have taken the bait and paid him a visit with his boys in tow. But the bad news is, the bloke who Shotgun Charlie blasted turns out to be Vince Connelly's cousin, King Arthur's nephew. Now, he's not really part of the family business, he was just having a Saturday afternoon flutter when we burst in, nevertheless King Arthur is calling for blood, and is not totally convinced it's down to the Morgans. For five years things have been amicable up there, the Morgans careful not to tread on King Arthur's toes, carving out their own territory without overlapping. And King Arthur knows they ain't got the muscle to take him on. So he can't quite figure out why they would suddenly come charging into one of his shops and shooting the place up.'

The Spaniard looked on thoughtfully. 'It was always going to be easier to bluff the cub than the wily old fox. But I guess it doesn't really matter now what he thinks. The impetuous cub has already done exactly what we wanted – provoked the Morgans into an all-out war, and that should keep Vince out of our hair,' he concluded.

The fight had started. Instead of his usual dancing around using speed to terrorise his opponents, Ali came out to the centre of the ring, stood flat footed, and unleashed an onslaught of jabs and combinations on Frazier, trying to finish him in the early rounds. By round five Ali was starting to tire, he had been over-confident and undertrained. Plus, the searing Philippine heat and a packed 25,000 capacity audience filling the suffocating Araneta Coliseum were all taking their toll on him.

'Look, he's fucked,' said Pete the Pig, taking another bite of his pickled egg and a handful of greasy chips for good measure.

'Hang on, Pete, don't write him off yet, and get your hands off my haddock,' replied Tel-Boy.

'So, where was I?' The Spaniard asked Harry over all the noise of the TV and a very excitable Pete the Pig.

'You were saying we need to look after this hotshot councillor, get him on side.'

'Yeah, that's right. I need you to take care of it tomorrow, H.'

'Well, where shall I go?' Harry asked.

'Take him down Simpsons-In-The-Strand, give him a little treat. Wine and dine him a bit, put on the airs and graces. I'll get there as soon as I can but I've gotta go down to Billericay first and pick up that consignment of German porn.'

'How am I going to keep him entertained?' inquired Harry. 'What am I going to chat to him about till you arrive? Tel-Boy says he's a woolly woofter, isn't he?'

'Just tell him he's sitting in the same seat as Oscar Wilde did when he used to dine there. These queers love all that shit.'

'You can tell him how you met Charles Dickens there,' chipped in Tel-Boy.

'I may be old, but I can still give you a back-hander, you cheeky sod,' Harry threatened Tel-Boy.

'I read one of his books once,' announced Pete the Pig, in between mouthfuls of chips. The other three looked at him in amazement.

'You read Charles Dickens?' Harry asked with incredulity.

'Yeah, it was very good, as it happens,' Pete the Pig said, finishing off his sausage in batter. 'It was all about an orphan who is always hungry and asking for more food. Then he becomes a pick-pocket and gets shot. Can't really remember the end. You not eating that pea fritter, boss?' he asked The Spaniard, who in turn was also staring at him dumbfounded.

'Anyway, getting back to what I was saying,' The Spaniard continued, addressing Harry, while slapping Pete the Pig's hand off his pea fritter. 'Put on a bit of show. This councillor can get planning for almost anything… at the right price. I'm sure he will be very useful to John Blackwood and his construction partners, but I want us to be the go-betweens, so don't mention any names. If we can broker a deal between them for a go-ahead on those old warehouses down London Bridge, we'll be on right little earner.'

'Cor, fuck me, look at the state of Frazier, he can hardly see,' shouted Tel-Boy. It was now round twelve, Frazier had come back and won the middle rounds, but was now being punished by a renewed Ali. Frazier's left eye was completely closed, and his right was just a puffy slit. It had been a bitter, bruising battle, but now Ali had found a reserve tank of energy. In round thirteen, he landed another punch on Frazier, knocking his mouthguard into the audience, and by round fourteen it was all over, Frazier's trainer stopping the fight.

'Yeah, not bad, I suppose,' concluded Pete the Pig as he stood up. 'It's the old one-two combination,' he said, feigning a couple of punches towards Tel-Boy before tripping over his Watney's party seven and landing face down in the remainder of his chips.

2005

Ignacio sat watching an interesting Channel 4 report on the state of the shadow Tory party. The news was full of the upcoming general election. The current ruling Labour party was looking for its third term in government, a fact that didn't really interest Ignacio one way or the other. He had little time for politicians in general, 'Just a bunch of squabbling spoilt schoolboys,' according to him. 'Scoring points off each other, especially if one was caught with his trousers down.' Which seemed to be happening more and more these days. The once youthful and grinning face of the current prime minister was now appearing everywhere, looking more tense and desperate than ever before. Beads of perspiration and two messy wars hung over him. Ignacio had once met him at some charity bash. Actually, in fairness, Ignacio had quite liked him. He could see they shared conviction and self-determination. They were both forceful, but charming with it. Ignacio had shared a joke with him about the deputy prime minister suffering from flatulence when over indulging at the buffet table.

But it was the current leader of the shadow party who interested Ignacio this evening, or, to be more precise, what he was hinting at. Should his party not get elected into government, he might well stand down as party leader. There were four likely candidates to replace him in the job should this happen, and Ignacio was quite well acquainted with the favourite front runner. He decided it might be a very opportune time to write a long-overdue letter. A letter that might well put the cat amongst the pigeons.

1975

'Why don't you come back to the Club for a couple of drinks,' The Spaniard said, putting his arm behind the councillor, and giving him a hearty pat on the back. It had been a long liquid lunch. Harry had done wonders keeping the councillor amused with all his old stories on the history of Soho and some of its more notorious and salacious residents. The Spaniard had joined them very late, and now the councillor was more than a little inebriated.

'Why not?' he replied jovially. 'Maybe we can pop into one of your porn shops that Harry's been telling me all about?' He winked at The Spaniard.

'We can do better than that, if you like?' answered The Spaniard. 'Let's drop by one of the sex joints... if you're up for it?' he grinned, nodding towards the councillor's crotch.

'Well, erm.. is it all strictly girls you deal in? It's just that I heard you could fix up all sorts of things,' the councillor asked tentatively.

The Spaniard looked across at Harry and they shared a knowing glance. 'You just tell me whatever it is you fancy, and I will find someone to tickle it. You can call it a little sweetener to the deal we just agreed on this afternoon.'

Now The Spaniard had him exactly where he wanted. The little business they had concluded would enable The Spaniard's associate – John Blackwood, to get the planning he needed to convert the warehouses into forty riverview loft apartments. This was going to be a big payday for everyone involved, including the councillor. But The Spaniard was never one to let an opportunity pass. In return for a hefty backhander, he knew the councillor would play his part – ensuring Blackwood Construction won the bidding for the land over its two better known rivals, plus turning a blind eye to any irregularities on Blackwood's plans. But The Spaniard wanted the councillor inextricably tied in, not just for this venture, but also any future enterprises he may need help with. The fact that the councillor had a penchant for young homosexual men provided the perfect snare.

Hence, within an hour of arriving at Club Bohemia a young, long-fair-haired, pretty-looking Russian boy named Dimitri, had been rounded up, and was now on the receiving end of the councillor's clumsy and reckless groping at the corner of the bar.

The councillor usually managed to keep his rather rash and sometimes impulsive streak in check. However the mix of too much alcohol, the relaxed surroundings of Club Bohemia and its seemingly liberal attitude to its patrons desires, fuelled his rebellious mood.

Another hour passed, and the councillor's insatiable appetite for Dimitri, and all that this young, firm stallion could provide was reaching its peak. A few words were shared between the councillor and his host, and shortly afterwards Tel-Boy had waved down a cab outside, and the councillor was being poured into the back, assisted by the very accommodating Dimitri.

'Come on slide over here' drawled the councillor, patting the seat next to him. 'You and I are going to have some fun.'

Dimitri smiled shyly. 'Where are we going?'

'I thought we could continue the party back at my place, maybe get to know each other even better,' answered the councillor with a raise of his eyebrows.

'You would like that, wouldn't you,' he continued with a sly grin.

Dimitri lolled on the back seat next to him, splaying his legs. The crotch of his jeans at full stretch, hugging the contours of their bulging contents. The councillor eyed him hungrily.

'Driver, Fulham Broadway,' said the councillor while rubbing his hand firmly on Dimitri's tight denim-clad thigh.

The phone ringing endlessly woke Maggie up. She glanced at the clock on the Goblin Teasmade. It was 5.25am. She knew no one would call her at that hour, and gave The Spaniard a prod, but got no response. She gave him another harder poke, and picked the phone up while he was stirring, and placed it next to his head on the pillow without bothering to inquire who it was.

'Hello, hello!' came a very frantic voice over the receiver.

The Spaniard picked it up. 'Yes, who is this?' he asked rather gruffly.

It was the councillor. 'I think he's dead, he's not moving, I can't wake him at all. It was only a few pills, just some uppers, that's all. Sorry, I don't know who else to call.'

'Alright, alright, calm down. What's your address? I'll come over, just hold tight, and don't call anybody else.' The Spaniard spoke in a very reassuring tone. Almost too calm and reassuring, thought the councillor, who was struggling desperately to keep a grip and not have a total breakdown. He gave The Spaniard his address and sat waiting for him, his nerves shot to pieces. This would surely be the end of him. All that hard work down the toilet. He had always taken risks, even as a kid he would

90

always push things to the limit. Seeing how far he could test the teachers before they snapped and driving his mother to tears with his disobedience. And then stealing things, not because he particularly wanted them, but because he loved the excitement and thrill of doing it. His parents had almost given up on him. They just couldn't understand why their bright, well-cared-for son would behave in such a manner.

After leaving school, things seemed to change. He settled down and began working hard, driven by money and craving success. But he still felt the urge to be reckless on occasion – taking bribes and indulging in secret lewd homosexual activities were just part of that. Feeding his darker side, it was almost as though he had two personae. A good, clean, morally decent public one, and a secret and far more sinister private one. He accepted and justified this to himself, by thinking that he wouldn't have achieved so much while still only in his mid twenties without this split personality. It drove his ambition and enabled him to fly by the seat of his pants if necessary. Life was all about risks, and those who were prepared to take more were often well rewarded, but it took a particular type of person to take them. Normally he got a real kick out of throwing caution to the wind, or stretching boundaries, as he liked to call it. But now this, this was more than reckless, this was bloody catastrophic. Bad enough explaining a dead body in your flat, but a fifteen-year-old dead rentboy with a stomach full of drugs? Now he was well and truly fucked.

The Spaniard turned up at 6.15am and listened to the councillor's rather embarrassed and frightened account of what had taken place that previous evening. The sex had been rough, brutal even. There were marks on Dimitri's wrists and neck where he had been tied to some old metal hooks in the fireplace. They had both been popping pills and drinking, and the councillor had encouraged Dimitri to take more to heighten the feeling of sexual ecstasy. The councillor had then fallen into an exhausted sleep for a couple of hours, and when he awoke dazed and dehydrated, he found Dimitri collapsed on the bathroom floor face down in his own vomit.

With remarkable control and showing minimal emotion, The Spaniard calmly made them both a cup of tea and then made a phone call to someone called Marvellous Magnus the Magician, so called because he could make things disappear, bodies being a speciality. Marvellous Magnus the Magician turned up at 8am in full clown's outfit, with red-and-yellow-checked penguin suit, top hat, and red nose.

'Morning, Magnus, how are you?' greeted The Spaniard.

'I'm alright, it's the others,' chuckled Magnus as he let off two short blasts on his pocket air horn.

'What the fuck was that?' screamed the councillor, close to having a nervous breakdown. 'What are you exactly? A children's entertainer?' he asked in horror.

'No, I'm a doctor. I just clown around in my spare time! Get it? Clown around!' guffawed Magnus, letting off another blast on the horn, sending the councillor scurrying to the kitchen cupboard and pouring himself a large brandy.

'How's tricks then?' smiled The Spaniard at his own pun.

'Not brilliant,' replied Magnus, suddenly looking quite depressed. 'To be honest, things just aren't the same. There's hardly any call for disposing of dead bodies nowadays. Ever since the Krays went down, business has been right slow. I don't know what the world's coming to,' he sighed wearily.

'Yeah, but you're still doing the magic shows, kiddie playgroups, and all the other things, aren't you?' assured The Spaniard.

'Yeah, but it ain't nowhere near as lucrative as stashing a stiff, is it?' complained Magnus. 'Give me a blood-spattered corpse over a snot-covered child any day.'

By 10am the body had been chopped into six individual pieces – the head, each hand, the trunk, and the two legs all separated from each other. The teeth in the decapitated head were then smashed one by one with a hammer, and the two hands were dropped in a container of acid to make identifying the dearly departed more difficult. Each limb was then packaged up and removed by Marvellous Magnus in his ice cream van – strawberry surprise being his speciality. The councillor closed his front door and collapsed on his sofa as the cheery chimes of the ice cream van faded down the road.

'You need to straighten this place out, and yourself too, for that matter!' The Spaniard warned as he finished his seventh cup of tea and started to head for the front door. 'It's not going to be cheap to clear up this little mess, it's not easy getting rid of bodies. And you are going to have to harden up, my son, if you want all this to go away without upsetting your cosy little life. Don't talk to no one about this... and I mean nobody, ever, you understand?'

'Yes, I understand,' came a very feeble reply.

'I will be in touch. Oh... and one last thing,' said The Spaniard as he opened the door and put his mug of tea down, 'you wanna stop drinking this muck, and get yourself some decent tea, remember *You only get an 'OO' with Typhoo!*'

2005

A sprightly, almost youthful-looking Percival Davenport leant back on his chair and extended his crossed legs up onto his desk. The election had been a disaster, or so the rest of his party thought. For the first time in their history, the opposing Labour party had just won its third consecutive term in power, albeit with a dramatically reduced majority. Percival's Tory party had managed to secure thirty-three new seats, but had still failed to attract what the media had called a rather disenchanted electorate. For the first time since 1929 none of the parties had received over ten million votes, many of the British public not bothering to turnout. But none of this could dampen Percival's spirits. In fact, it was the perfect result for him. The old man would be forced to step down from leader now, making way for Percival to ascend to his rightful position. Then he could sit back and wait, watching the increasing unpopularity of the current labour government as voters lost their stomach for war. The body count from Iraq and Afghanistan was growing by the day, the pressure mounting on the government to call for another election, which they surely could not win for a fourth time. By then the public would be clamouring to get them out and vote in Percival Davenport as their new conservative prime minister.

'Morning, Percival!' Polly entered the office carrying his usual skinny latte. 'You're looking very cheerful today, what were you up to last night?' she smiled.

'Wouldn't you like to know, you nosy little thing?' Percival replied, smiling back. Actually, it was just as well she didn't know, otherwise any plans to be the next prime minister would be well and truly scuppered.

'Here's your post,' she said. 'There's a very neat handwritten one on top marked private and personal.'

'Well, I hope you haven't opened it then, Ms Efficient,' Percival replied as he took the pile from her. Not that he minded her opening his mail, he got so much of it that it was a godsend to have someone like Polly taking care of the more mundane stuff. And to give her her due, she was pretty good at knowing what she should and shouldn't open.

'Thanks, Polly. I'm going up to see the old man at nine, shouldn't be too long.'

'Sizing up his office already?' joked Polly. 'You have to win the leadership election first, you know,' she warned.

'Just a formality, Polly, a mere formality,' he replied, brimming with confidence.

'It's all confirmed. The councillor has got the planning permission through for the old warehouses down London Bridge. I've been on the blower to John Blackwood, he's well chuffed. He will be able to start construction in a month's time. He wanted to know where and when to give you the pay-off. I told him to come into the club tonight and have a chat directly with you.'

'Terrific. Thanks, Harry,' smiled The Spaniard, clapping his hands together. 'I reckon we should use this dough to get those premises round on Wardour Street. It would make a great little porn shop, being just off Oxford Street. All those Selfridges shoppers can pop in for their Swedish penis pumps and kinky handcuffs.'

Peggy looked up from her dusting. 'He could do with one of those Swedish enhancer things,' she said, nodding her head at Harry. 'I've seen bigger willies on an Action Man,' she continued, waggling her little finger in the air.

'Yes, thank you, my little nest of vipers!' replied Harry. 'As I recall, you never used to complain when it was time for a bit of toad-in-the-hole.'

'Toad-in-the-hole! More like find the blinkin' hole,' scoffed Peggy. 'Last time you went anywhere near it, there was a king on the throne.'

'Well, maybe if you made yourself slightly more alluring, dear, the old magic might reappear.' Harry turned to The Spaniard. 'You've never seen anything like it. She wears the biggest *Alan Whickers* you've ever seen. I can't work out whether they come up to her nipples or her nipples droop down to them.'

'Oh, 'have a word with yourself,' Peggy clucked. 'You're the one with droopy old knackers.'

'How long you two been married now?' interrupted The Spaniard, chuckling to himself.

'Forty-two long years,' answered Harry. 'The Krays only got thirty.'

'Well, I dunno why I stayed with him so long,' Peggy said, shaking her head. 'Do you know, when I was pregnant with our first one – little Shirley – I said to him then, I said, I'm pregnant, you don't want it, and you don't want me. I might as well throw myself off Blackfriars Bridge. And do you know what that shit said to me? He said, Peggy, not only are you a terrific fuck, but you're a bloody good sport, too!'

Harry could sense that Peggy was just getting started, and thought it high time he lightened the mood before he faced a large portion of cold shoulder for the next two days. 'Come on, my little munchkin, let's not go over all that now. You know how much I love you.' He turned to The Spaniard. 'You know, I'm so used to her now, I could never leave her.'

'Shame!' Peggy muttered, as she stubbed out the cigarette that Harry had just lit for himself.

'It would be like losing a leg,' Harry continued.

'Humph!' came a very unimpressed sigh from Peggy as she headed towards the office door.

'You see, she's everything to me,' Harry continued in all sincerity to The Spaniard. 'Every old sock needs an old shoe, and Peg is my old shoe.' As Peggy closed the door behind her, she allowed herself a secret contented smile from Harry's last words.

'And that's why you should take care of Maggie,' Harry started on The Spaniard now. 'She's a real good'un, that one, a lovely girl. And in your line of work you will be lucky to find someone who will put up with all the ups and downs and stick with you. Take the advice of an old man who's seen far too much aggro and hate during his time. If you find something precious, protect and love it, because that will provide you with strength when you're old.'

'I know, H, you're right. And I do love Maggie, but it don't matter what I do, I can feel her slipping away from me. I give her everything a girl could want, but that doesn't seem to satisfy her.'

'Well, maybe it's not always the material things that a girl wants?' Harry said quietly. But he could see The Spaniard wasn't interested in continuing the conversation.

'Anyway, getting back to this John Blackwood business, how much you giving the councillor for his part?' Harry asked.

'Well, I've been thinking about that, what with that whole Dimitri fiasco I figure he owes me,' replied The Spaniard.

'True, you've really got him by the short and curlies. I'm sure he will be bending over backwards for you now... well, hopefully not in the proverbial sense,' laughed Harry.

'The thing is, H, I think we should keep that little episode back for a rainy day,' The Spaniard said thoughtfully. 'I mean, it was a bit of a bonus, the councillor getting all kinky on us. Who'd of thought he would tie the kid up and shove pills down his neck. What a turn up for the books. 'I think we should just pay him his percentage as agreed for now, and not mention the Dimitri thing. Let him think that we are his pals and that we will protect him. Then one day when we need a big favour, something far more tricky or expensive to get past the council, that's when we play our trump card.'

'Sounds sensible,' agreed Harry. 'Is the Dimitri thing all squared off?' he asked.

'Yeah, that wasn't too difficult. Turns out he's got no family, apart from a younger brother called Nikolai. They've been in and out of foster homes all their lives. Dimitri's been hustling on the streets since he turned thirteen. Anyway Tel-Boy tracked down this Nikolai and told him some yarn how Dimitri had met some wealthy actor who has taken him off to the south of France while he is shooting a film there. Tel-Boy slipped him a wad of notes, said it was from Dimitri and he was really onto a good thing, but he couldn't name the actor because he is so far in the closet not even his own mother knows, let alone Pinewood Studios.'

'Good old Terry, some imagination that boy's got,' grinned Harry. 'So, lastly, what we doing with Dirty Bertie? We got some great snaps of him with those two girls all dressed up in their school uniforms. The randy old goat wants us to find another eight of them for some private party he's giving down on his country estate next month. I told him you would be in touch.'

'Fine, I'll call him tonight. Just keep the photos secure in the safe. There's no hurry, we can afford to build up a nice little portfolio of his Lordship's mucky habits, and then seek payment when the time is right. OK, I've gotta fly now, it's Maggie's birthday, and she's got a babysitter lined up. I promised I would take her to the pictures.'

'Yeah, what you going to see?' asked Harry.

'I'm not sure. It's just been released. I think she said something about a giant killer shark that keeps eating everybody.'

'Mmm… sounds cheerful. Whatever happened to all the lovely old romantic movies, a bit of Fred Astaire and Ginger Rogers flying down to Rio? Nobody had to get eaten or shot back then.'

'Times are changing, H, times are changing. Did you see they shot that record breaker man – Ross McWhirter – the other day. The bloody IRA, right outside his own home, shot him in the head at close range. No one's safe any more, H, it's a violent society out there. Nowadays watching a shark taking a nibble out of a few surfers is light entertainment. Ta-ta for now.'

2005

As he walked past Polly's desk on his way into his own office, Percival called back, 'Polly, I'm popping down the Strangers Bar in the commons around midday, a little celebratory drink.' His face was the duplicate of a fat Cheshire cat who had just cleaned Cadbury's out of cream. The old man had given him the nod, he was stepping down as leader of the opposition and firmly giving Percival his full backing to take over. Percival plonked himself down in his iconic Charles Eames chair and pulled out the little package of white powder from his breast pocket. He then selected his Harvey Nichols store card from the numerous other credit cards in his over-stretched wallet. He divided and efficiently chopped the powder into two slim lines with the panache of Michelangelo adding the finishing touches to the Sistine Chapel ceiling. And then with a tightly rolled crisp fifty-pound note, he snorted a line up each greedy little nostril. He then picked up his samurai steel letter opener, a gift from the Japanese Foreign Minister during a recent visit. Even the Japs recognised who should be next in charge of this once great island nation. He picked up the handwritten envelope that Polly had put aside and sliced it open in one sharp precise movement.

Dear Percy

May I be one of the first to congratulate you on what I'm sure will be your new position of power. Unlike your party colleagues, I'm certain you won't see your recent loss in the election as anything more than a slight hindrance. You may have lost the battle but certainly not the war! If I'm correct it will only be a few days before a change of leadership within your party will be called for. Someone more modern, energetic, and ambitious to lead the Tories forward. And who could be better than the young councillor who rose through the ranks of local government, backbenchers, and into the Shadow Cabinet with such critical acclaim.

Naturally, like any person of power I'm sure there have been ups and downs along the way, both professional and personal. And it's so often the personal ones that come back to haunt us. Surely everyone should be forgiven for a youthful misdemeanour, but unfortunately the British public can be very harsh when it comes to politics. The slightest whiff of scandal, and they want to see absolute humiliation and a damn good flogging.

I will be having a lunchtime drink in the Black Jack, Peckham, a week on Monday. Why don't you pop by and have a pint with an old friend? Catch up on old times, talk about past Russian acquaintances that are sadly no longer with us.

Your friend

Ignacio Perez

The Spaniard.

The letter fell to the floor, and perspiration dripped down the back of his neck, seeping under his Thomas Pink collar. He stared down at the shining silver samurai steel letter opener still in his hand. He could end it all now, an honourable death. That's it, he could commit *seppuku*. Maybe he should do it during Prime Minister's question time. That would wipe the smug smiles off all those frontbench arseholes.

'The honourable gentleman for Islington South and Finsbury appears to have disembowelled himself.'

No, that was not even an option, he would never give them the satisfaction of seeing the cool Percival Davenport crumble. And as for that bloody Spaniard, could he really be out there after all this time, still running his extortion, racketeering and violent operations? He must be an old man by now, a weak old man... a weak and disposable old man. The more he thought about it, the initial shock and chilling words of the letter left him and were replaced with a rush of adrenalin. His veins pumped with electricity, a wave of euphoria washed over him, just as it always did when he was about to step out of the comfort zone. The letter, the risk of being exposed, the need to find a way to silence The Spaniard, all gave him a tremendous thrill.

'Oh yes, Ignacio, my old friend, we shall meet, but it will be Percival Davenport that prevails.'

1975

The Spaniard sat staring out of the cafe window before ordering a second egg and bacon bap.

'Go easy on the grease this time, Joe,' he called.

Joe gave him an old-fashioned look. 'If you don't like it, there's always the Wimpy bar down the road. None of my other customers are complaining.'

'Joe, you don't have any other customers.'

'Well, that's as may be, but I don't come down your porn shop and complain your dildos are too small.'

'Joe, just cook the fucking bap, eh?'

'OK, OK! Do you want mushrooms in it?' Joe asked, while simultaneously removing something green from his left nostril and flicking it in the direction of the mushrooms bubbling in the fat.

'Tell you what, Joe, I've gone right off the idea now. I'll just have another cup of tea instead.'

'Make your bloody mind up, mate,' Joe called over his shoulder as he shuffled back behind the counter and turned up the radio.

'We interrupt The Golden Hour with Tony Blackburn for this latest newsflash. It is being confirmed that Saigon has fallen into the hands of the North Vietnamese army, and the last of the American diplomatic, military, and civilian personnel are being evacuated by helicopter. After sixteen long years of fighting, which saw many other surrounding Asian nations drawn in, it is believed that the total loss of military and civilian life is estimated to be over 4.5 million. There are also reports that the communist regime – The Khmer Rouge – have taken control of Phnom Penh in Cambodia. Their leader Pol Pot, or Brother Number One as he refers to himself, has ordered *the evacuation of all urban areas and declared Year Zero. We will have more in our lunchtime news bulletin at midday.'*

'Thanks, John, back to the music, folks. This is Tony Blackburn and what year did this get to number three in the charts?'

'Bloody commie bastards,' muttered Joe over the sound of spitting fat and T. Rex's '20th Century Boy'.

The bell above the cafe door chimed as an overweight perspiring Detective Chief Inspector walked in. 'Morning!' He nodded at The Spaniard.

'Hello, Eddie, you're looking a little hot under the collar,' greeted The Spaniard.

'So would you be if you'd just walked the length of Wandsworth Road. That stupid scrotum Sykes parked the Granada at the wrong end. He reckoned this place was at the Vauxhall end. He promised the Deputy Commissioner he could pick up tickets for the Cricket World Cup at The Oval, little fuckin' brown nose. In the meantime, yours truly has to trek halfway across south bleedin' London. Anyway, what's the grub like in here? I'm ravenous,' he asked.

'It's surprisingly good,' smiled The Spaniard. 'I highly recommend the full Monty, especially the mushrooms.'

The DCI ordered his breakfast at the counter then plonked his ample weight on the orange PVC bench opposite The Spaniard.

'So, how's tricks, Eddie?' asked The Spaniard.

'Mustn't grumble, my son, mustn't grumble.'

DCI Eddie Mullins was fifty-four years of age and knew everything that went on in his patch. By his rotund figure it was easy to detect that he had more than a healthy appetite, but he also liked dipping his fingers in lots of other pies, not just the steak and kidney variety.

He was one of the most corrupt cops on the force, but also one of the most feared and respected. His nickname was Edward the Confessor, on account that it didn't matter whether you did the crime or not, once you were in that interview room with him you would confess to anything. The Spaniard and Edward the Confessor had known each other for five years now. They shared a professional relationship of mutual courtesy in return for the odd snippet of information. Neither one trusted the other completely, but they were both very much aware of how useful they were to each other.

'How's that lovely girl of yours?' asked Eddie.

'What? Maggie? Yeah she's fine, thanks,' replied The Spaniard.

'I saw her down Knightsbridge the other day. She's a stunner, that one, you wanna look after her.'

'Yeah, I do, thank you very much,' said The Spaniard, slightly irritated. 'Funny, someone else said that to me the other day. So anyway, what did you want to chat to me about?'

Eddie chuckled. 'Patience, patience, my son. It's always the same with you. Can't a couple of generals sit down and take time out for a cuppa and chew the fat?'

'Generals? That's a curious term,' inquired The Spaniard.

'Well yes... generals. We both have our merry little band of soldiers, ready to do the dirty work once we give the order.'

'I'm sorry, I'm not sure I'm with you,' The Spaniard said, shaking his head.

The DCI gave out another chuckle. 'Oh, come on now, no need to be modest. Everyone knows half the criminal fraternity of London would jump if you told them to. Take Shotgun Charlie for example...' The DCI trailed off.

'I would rather not, thank you very much. Anyway, what's that twat got to do with me?' asked The Spaniard.

'Ooh, had a lover's tiff, have we?'

'No.' The Spaniard said firmly.

'Really? That's not what I heard,' the DCI smiled. 'I heard that Shotgun Charlie is not happy at all with you. In fact he's been going around the manor saying you're chicken. No, sorry, it wasn't chicken. What was it? Ah yes, custard, that's it, custard. Because you're yellow and run. Now why would one of your foot soldiers say something like that?'

The Spaniard leant back in his chair and gave the DCI a long hard look. 'I'm not sure, Eddie, you're the detective, you tell me.'

'Mmm... not bad. You're right about these mushrooms, egg's a bit greasy, though,' said the DCI dipping a soggy chip into his runny egg yolk. 'Just a thought,' he continued, 'but I'm wondering whether it's got something to do with a little blag in Birmingham. Where four fella's have half-inched the takings from two bookies and had it away on their tiptoes.'

'Cor, fuck me, Eddie, you ought to be in goal for West Ham, They'd be top of the league by now. Does nothing get past you?'

'Ah, so you did have something to do with that stunt?'

'No, Eddie, I didn't say that, did I? All I heard was that someone turned over a bookies, and Shotgun Charlie's name was in the frame.'

'OK, play it your way, my son. You know I'm not coming after you. It's no skin off my nose what you get up to outside of my patch. But you need to keep a grip on those monkeys that work for you. It's bad for business having the likes of Charlie McCray blabbing at the mouth. It's already got the attention of the station super, and phone calls are being made between him and the nick in Birmingham. Now I might be putting two and two together and coming up with five, but if you've got the Connelly clan coming after you, make sure it's not on my turf. Because if it is, I won't be able to protect you. Don't shit on my doorstep, my son. Oh, at bloody last, that scrotum Sykes has found it, miracles will never cease.'

The Spaniard glanced out of the window and saw the blue Ford Granada Ghia pull up outside.

'Thanks for the breakfast. You can pick up the tab. Be lucky, my son.' The DCI slurped down the rest of his tea and then lumbered out of the cafe.

2005

'You're looking ravishing this morning, Roxanne,' Ignacio smiled, as he approached the betting shop counter.

'Yeah, whatever!' Roxanne grunted back.

'Tenner each way on Bohemian Rhapsody please.' Ignacio pushed the money and betting slip through the glass window.

Roxanne flicked her purple fringe to one side, revealing two heavily made-up eyes with enough mascara to sink a battleship, and a nose piercing the size of a Malteser. 'You sure, Ignacio? It's 16-1, it's a donkey, mate.'

'We'll see, I've got a good feeling about it. I used to have a club called Bohemia.'

'Well, whatever! You're the punter, I s'pose,' she replied, feeding the slip into the machine.

'Excuse me, did I hear right, are you Ignacio?'

'Yep. Do I know you?' Ignacio asked the scruffy-looking woman who had approached him.

'Ignacio Perez? The one they used to call The Spaniard?'

'Well, yes, but that was a long time ago. Now I guess I'm just plain Ignacio,' he said smiling, unprepared for the mouthful of saliva that the woman spat straight in his face.

'You fucking bastard! I knew I would find you one day,' she screamed.

Ignacio grabbed her by the arm. 'Hey, hey calm down,' he said, slightly bewildered, but increasing his steel-like grip. 'Who are you?'

'You don't remember me? Well, why would you? You never cared about anyone else, apart from yourself. I'm Charlie's widow.'

'Charlie?' Ignacio asked, racking his brains for someone he knew called Charlie.

'Yeah, Shotgun Charlie, remember? You murdering bastard. I'm Molly McCray.' She then stamped hard on Ignacio's gout-ridden foot, causing him to yelp with agony and release his grip on her. This gave her enough time to get out of the door. He went after her, but she had already got into a waiting car. As the driver was about to pull away, Ignacio grabbed hold of the passenger door and managed to prise it open, but the car was starting to accelerate. Molly McCray shouted through the open door 'Your day will come, you murderer, I will find you again.'

Ignacio was no longer able to hang on. She pulled the door closed, leaving Ignacio tripping and falling in the road as the car sped off.

1975

Shotgun Charlie cracked open another can of Long Life beer and flicked on the television.

'And now, live from Norwich, it's the quiz of the week, with your host Nicholas Parsons.'

'Aw, fuck me, not Sale of the fucking Century again,' swore Charlie. He flicked over to the BBC, just in time to catch the end of his favourite programme, 'Dad's Army'. He flopped back on the mustard coloured corduroy sofa and put his feet up on his son's space hopper.

Pike was singing: 'Whistle while you work, Hitler is a twerp. He's half barmy, so's his army, whistle while you work.'

Shotgun Charlie started chuckling, he didn't hear the latch slip on his front door.

The German U-Boat Captain: 'Your name will also go on the list. What is it?'

'Don't tell him, Pike,' shouted Captain Mainwaring.

Shotgun Charlie was now roaring with laughter. He raised his hand to wipe the tears from his eyes, just as the hammer came pounding down, hard, on his skull. The first two blows caused massive damage, but the third blow was the fatal one, smashing the parietal bone, rupturing the brain. His body convulsed before flopping sideways on the blood-splattered sofa, which now resembled a giant jam sponge.

Two days later, when The Spaniard arrived home in Earls Court there was no sign of Maggie. He went upstairs to their bedroom and noticed how the dressing table looked so bare without Maggie's personal possessions spread out on it. Her hair brush, face cream, Arpège perfume, and the shell she had collected from Woolacombe beach, all absent. He threw open the double wardrobe doors and was faced with a large empty space where once Maggie's favourite dresses had hung next to his Gieves and Hawkes suits. The large jewellery box was no longer on the shelf. He turned and went into his son's bedroom. Most of the Lego bricks and farmyard animals were still lying on the floor, but the shelf reserved for Elvis – the beloved teddy – was now empty. The Spaniard leapt down the stairs two at a time and went back into the kitchen. It was only then that he noticed the copy of the *Evening Standard* open on the table, and a handwritten note next to it.

The headline read: *'Body of local villain found bludgeoned to death in Hackney flat.'*

The scribbled note read: *'If you really care about us as much as you say you do, then you will let us go.'*

2005

It was a beautiful, bright sunny day, and Pepe felt upbeat and optimistic as he and Samir pulled up in the hospital car park. The present round of chemo treatment had finished yesterday, and Pepe was hoping to see some marked improvement. When they got to the ward, Pepe's mum was sitting up in bed trying to do the *Times* crossword. This was a challenge that she had regularly completed before her illness, but now, under the strain of the cancer and the traumatic treatment, her strength of mind and overall ability to concentrate was reduced to a fraction of its previous power. The newspaper kept slipping from her grip, and Pepe could see only two clues pencilled in. She looked exhausted and drained of colour. The once beautiful long flowing golden hair had been stolen by chemotherapy, leaving just a few loose wispy strands. The big twinkling green eyes that could melt anyone's heart were now sunken hollows, underlined by dark rings. But as Pepe and Samir walked in, they were still greeted by the warmest and most affectionate smile for both of them.

'Hello, my little soldiers,' she called.

'Hello, Maggie,' they both said in unison.

She gave out a raspy chuckle. 'You two, you're like a couple of odd twins.'

'I know,' said Pepe. 'He's the black me.'

'Well, does that make you the gay me?' laughed Samir.

'Oh, it's good to see you both, my darling boys.' Maggie smiled, struggling to hold out a hand to them.

'Boys? Mum, we're thirty-three years old.'

'And high court judges,' piped in Samir.

When she had first started taking care of little Samir, while his father Winnie had been at work, he had called her Auntie Maggie. But she thought that made her sound too old, so she suggested that he should just call her Maggie. Then because his little friend was calling her Maggie, and Pepe wanted to copy everything his little friend did, he stopped calling her Mummy and called her Maggie, too. At first she found this a little disturbing, but then it grew on her. Every day she stood at the school gates waiting for her little scamps to come tearing out of the classroom and run across the school playground shouting 'Maggie, Maggie!' In a strange way it made her feel extra special. And like all habits, it stuck, and as Pepe got older it became even more endearing, their relationship surpassing that of a regular mother and son. Instead, a great friendship between them evolved. There were very few secrets Pepe kept from Samir, but if there were any, you could be sure that the only person who would know them would be Maggie.

'How's it going, then, Maggie?' Samir asked, trying to sound bright under the circumstances.

'Oh, marvellous, darling, right barrel of laughs it is in here,' she replied, raising her eyebrows. 'Haven't seen hide nor hair of a doctor since I arrived. Her in the next bed does nothing but complain about her sore arse, and Nurse Ratched over there has the bedside manner of Boris Karloff.'

'Glad you're keeping your spirits up,' Pepe said, smiling, slipping his hand over hers and giving it a squeeze. 'So when are you coming out?' he asked.

'I don't know, my darling. I don't know if I can right now, I just feel so damn weak,' she smiled sadly at Pepe.

'But the treatment is finished, so we can get you out of here as soon as you're strong enough, can't we?' implored Pepe.

'Yes, darling.'

'Well, come on then, get yourself better. You don't want to be lying about in here for longer than necessary, do you?' urged Pepe. 'I want my Maggie back OK. Promise me you're going to get better… please?'

'I promise I will try.' Maggie managed an unconvincing wink.

'Good. Now why don't we finish this crossword together,' smiled Pepe. 'Hey, brains, feel free to chip in,' he said, nodding Samir's way.

'Oh no, not that wretched thing, I can't seem to think today,' Maggie said, shaking her head. 'Tell you what, do you think brains can go and find a couple of teas, there's something I have been meaning to talk to you about.'

Pepe's heart sank. Samir, thinking along the same lines as Pepe, jumped up, relieved that Maggie had given him an excuse to disappear while any bad news she had to pass onto Pepe was done in his absence.

'Don't look like that,' Maggie said, gripping Pepe's hand. 'What I have to tell you is not about me. Well, not directly. It's about your father.'

'My father? What do you suddenly want to talk about him for?' asked Pepe, more than a little stunned. 'You never wanted to talk about him before.'

'Well, maybe it's time I did. Maybe I was wrong not to tell you about him before. I have come to think that you have a right to know about him.'

'Good grief, Maggie you never cease to amaze me. I can't believe all those times when I was a kid, I begged you to talk about him, and now I'm in my thirties and gone past caring, you decide to tell me. I'm not sure I want to know. I haven't even thought about him since I was teenager, what's the point of telling me now?'

There was a long pause while they stared defiantly at each other. Eventually Maggie said, 'The reason I never wanted to talk about him before was because I was worried you would want to see him, and I couldn't stand that, it would have worried me sick.'

'Why?' Pepe asked testily.

'Well, your father wasn't what you would call a good man.'

'No shit, Sherlock. I guessed that a long time ago. He obviously didn't treat you too well, otherwise you wouldn't have walked out on him.'

'No, I don't mean good as in he was bad towards me. In actual fact, he always tried his best with me. I'm sure he loved me in his own way, and you too, for that matter. It's just that he was different, different from other men.'

'Go on, I'm all ears,' Pepe nodded, impatient to hear what his mother had hidden from him for so many years.

'Do you remember around 1986 when you were about fourteen? You cut out all those newspaper articles about a man called The Spaniard who was accused of murdering an ex-con on the Costa del Crime? The newspapers also referred to him as The Hammer, it was his nickname amongst his own kind. You were fixated with the story. For weeks you were fascinated by all the stuff the papers kept dragging up on him. Previous charges and allegations of violence hitting the headlines, and all the while Scotland Yard trying desperately to extradite him back from Malaga. It was scary, your obsession with him. It was as if you knew, like some sixth sense was telling you that this man was a part of you.'

'You're kidding, right? You were married to him? My dad was The Spaniard? The man who killed Maltese Tony? I don't believe it.' Pepe reeled.

Maggie smiled. 'No, we were never married, but yes, he is your father.'

'The Spaniard?' Pepe asked again incredulously.

'Yes, darling. Why do you think you're called Pepe? It certainly wasn't my idea to give you a Spanish name. Actually, if I'd had my way you'd be called Englebert, after Englebert Humperdinck. Such a wonderful voice, and lovely teeth.'

'Well, thank heavens for that. I'm glad The Hammer or whatever his name is, did something right by me. Englebert indeed! You're a flippin' fruitcake, Mother. Anyway, so why didn't you get married?'

'Oh, he wanted to, he asked me a couple of times. He even bought me a beautiful big diamond engagement ring. It had more carats than Bugs Bunny. I wanted to say yes. My heart told me yes, I really loved him in the beginning, but in my head there were doubts, alarm bells ringing at the back. There was something about him, Pepe, something that was not complete. He wasn't a psychopath, not like some of the papers said, nothing like that. They made him out to be some maniac, but how could I fall in love with a sociopath? Why would I have a child by someone like that? To me, he was kind and gentle, amusing even. He could be very charming, and he was very good looking, but I could see what he was capable of. Inside there was something very dark, sadistic even. He was very sociable, very magnetic, he would draw people to him.

Not just the dangerous criminals at the time, but also the rich and powerful, but always with a hidden motive. I imagined him as a lovely laughing happy little boy playing in a sunny garden, collecting all the different little insects – ladybirds, butterflies, beautiful creatures, and then the bees, the wasps, the beetles, the tougher creatures. Chatting and singing to them, while placing them all gently in a large matchbox. But when the sun goes down and it's time for bed, he waits till no one is looking, and instead of opening that matchbox and letting his little friends go free, he strikes a match and sets light to the corner of the matchbox. And with a wide smile watches them all burn.'

'Oh terrific! He sounds like a right barrel of laughs,' mocked Pepe.

Maggie looked hard into Pepe's face. 'He was good to me, and he adored you, but I didn't want you growing up in that kind of environment. As time went on, I knew he was getting more and more mixed up in violence and trouble. It was only a matter of time till something bad happened. It was too dangerous, I couldn't put you at risk. If he didn't wind up with a bullet in him, he would probably end up in Wormwood Scrubs. And I certainly didn't want to be one of those prisoners' wives, relying on the help of other hard men who owed Ignacio favours while he served time.'

'Ignacio?' Pepe questioned.

'Yes, that's his name. Ignacio. Not that anyone ever knew that back then, and if they did they would never dream of calling him it, apart from me. It was always The Spaniard. He kept it that way to conceal his real identity.'

Pepe nodded, feeling like he had just received a gift. Hearing his father's name, a name that only his mother used for him. It felt like he knew something intimate about this man. Even though he did not know him like others, it felt like he had an advantage over them; he shared a secret of his.

'So, if I remember correctly, he never went to prison?' asked Pepe.

'True, as far as I know, they never got him for anything,' Maggie replied. 'He always said he was far too smart for that. He had a saying – porridge is best left to the Scots and the witless. But that was back then, goodness only knows where he might be now. Either lording it up on a luxury yacht somewhere, or rotting in some gutter.'

'You have no idea where he is?'

'Where who is?' Samir asked, returning with the teas and a soggy-looking Bakewell tart.

'Nothing bro, you ain't gonna believe it,' frowned Pepe.

1975

Over the last couple of weeks, news had been filtering down to The Spaniard about the outbreak of violence between the Morgans and the Connelly Clan. A local reporter in Birmingham had picked up the story and had written a feature about the two families, exposing their grip on the racecourses, the protection money the bookies had to pay, and the beatings that were handed out to those foolish enough to defy the two families. But now the beatings were between the two rival factions. Both sides were receiving injuries, and poor Joe public was often getting caught in the middle of it. Local drinking haunts and clubs were being ambushed by each side in search of the other gang members. Vince Connelly wasn't content with just putting Gareth Morgan in a coma, he was after Taffy Morgan – the younger brother – too. King Arthur was trying to keep a lid on the whole thing, knowing that the publicity would bring the whole bloody lot of them down with an almighty thump. Even the senior bent coppers on their payroll wouldn't be able to save them if the aggro continued.

Sure enough, a week later the inevitable happened. A massive fight broke out at Hereford Racecourse, and three people were killed during the trouble. The course was part of the Morgan stronghold, and Vince Connelly and his men had turned up looking for Taffy Morgan. Fortunately for Taffy he was not there on this crowd-packed Saturday afternoon, but his son Rhys was. The brawl broke out down by the bookie stands and soon escalated into a full-blown riot. Broken bottles, stools, and placard boards were used as weapons against knives and baseball bats. The crowds ran screaming for cover as Prince Vince advanced against the Morgan brigade, stabbing Rhys Morgan to death, and causing two other casualties, one from each side, with fatal head wounds. It made front-page news on most of the tabloids the following day. The BBC interviewed the Midlands Chief Superintendent, asking what was to be done about protecting the public from such shocking events. It had gone too far, the powers that be were not happy, and pressure was on for the authorities to take action, examples were to be made and heads needed to roll.

2005

'No, let me, it's my shout,' Ignacio offered, beaming at Percival. 'A celebration is in order. I heard on the news this morning that you are now the official appointed leader of the Tory party. I'm surprised someone holding such a highly elevated position would be seen in such lowly surroundings, particularly with someone like me.' Ignacio winked.

'I feel I have little choice,' Percival said, through a taut smile. He was determined to remain cordial and relaxed, and not to allow this animal the satisfaction of seeing him intimidated or afraid of what hold he might have on him. He told himself to just play along, gather enough information of his own. Figure his moves and then outsmart him.

They sat in the corner of the snug bar in The Black Jack. Apart from a couple of old timers, the bar was empty, as Ignacio had known it would be. He didn't want to scare his prey away, not before he was firmly in his grasp. They chatted about the old days for a while, about when Percival was a young, ambitious councillor and already making senior decisions for the local borough council. Even someone with Percival's highly tuned determination and enterprise would struggle to be in such a key position nowadays. But it was very different back then in the seventies. Kids didn't spend years in further education, waiting till they were in their twenties before stepping into the employment arena. It was all apprenticeships at sixteen back then, or maybe spending another year getting a few 'A' Levels at college, then launching into a chosen career at the earliest opportunity. And what a career Percival

Davenport had made for himself, his focus firmly on running the whole country.

'I'm not interested in causing you any problems,' Ignacio spoke quietly. 'It's not my intention to hamper your progress, far from it. In actual fact, I think you would make a fine prime minister, not that I care much for politics myself, too much chat and not enough action, if you know what I mean?'

Percival certainly did know what he meant. Diplomacy not really a prominent feature of The Spaniard's skill set.

'What's good for you is good for me. Friends should share each other's success. I helped you in the early days, and now all I'm asking for is a token of your appreciation. An acknowledgement, or recognition for past favours.'

'Past favours? Or do you mean past favour singular?' Percival asked. 'I mean, are we talking about one favour in particular?'

'Well, now that you come to mention it,' The Spaniard nodded. 'There is one favour... One very big favour that springs to mind. Let's be honest, the removal and subsequent hush-up of a dead body is a pretty big favour by anyone's standards.'

'Can we keep our voices down a bit, please,' whispered Percival, suddenly becoming very uncomfortable. 'I thought our dealings back then were all very well reciprocated. We assisted each other. You certainly benefited financially from my help in passing certain plans expeditiously. Those that might otherwise have been blocked had they landed on anyone else's desk,' said Percival, slightly irritated.

'As did you... as did you, Percy, me old son. I never heard you complain about the kickbacks, your cut was always more than generous,' Ignacio said, fixing Percival with a menacing glare.

'I was not aware that I was still in debt to you in some way,' grumbled Percival.

The Spaniard paused. When he spoke again his tone had changed completely. Any hint of the previous friendliness, however insincere it may have been, was now dropped. 'Now listen to me, you pompous prat,' he snarled. 'I want a hundred grand, and if you know what's good for you you'll pay up pronto.'

'What?' Percival couldn't help letting out a cry of exclamation. Of course, he had been prepared for this. It was what he had expected. Even the amount was not far away from the sum he had anticipated. But just hearing The Spaniard saying it, no, demanding it, made it sound much worse. 'I can't just hand over that amount of money, I don't have it,' Percival said weakly.

'Oh, come on, Percy boy,' Ignacio said, switching back to a more conciliatory tone. 'We both know that's not true. I've done my homework. It's amazing what you can find in Debrett's and on the internet. I see you're a man of property. That's a pretty impressive portfolio you possess. If you don't have the lolly stuffed in a vault, I'm sure it wouldn't be too difficult to raise it with all those assets as collateral.'

'That would take time,' Percival replied adamantly.

'Well, unfortunately, Percy, time is not on your side. I want the dough by the end of the month, which gives you just shy of three weeks. Time enough, don't you think?'

'That really is not possible,' Percival said, shaking his head.

'Well then, you will just have to make it possible, won't you? Otherwise the headlines are going to read –

Davenport in Deadly Drugged Dalliance! Depending on how much of a story I decide to give the papers,' threatened Ignacio.

'Am I the only one?' asked Percival, changing tack suddenly, hoping to catch The Spaniard unaware.

'What do you mean, the only one?' Ignacio asked.

'I mean, I'm curious. Am I the only one you're blackmailing, or are there others? What about that Lord that used to grace your club, the one that liked younger girls?'

Percival had taken Ignacio by surprise. Ignacio was hesitating before answering, his face trying to remain impassive, but his eyes said it all. His expression belying his answer when he replied with an unconvincing, 'No.'

'I'm sure there must be others like me with skeletons in their closets that maybe you are privy to,' suggested Percival. 'Is it possible you may even having damning evidence? Photos perhaps?'

Ignacio remained tight-lipped, unsure of Percival's motive with this questioning.

Percival was certain he now had an ally, a very rich and powerful ally, who like him would want nothing more than the demise of this Spanish pariah. He just wanted to hear The Spaniard say it, just needed confirmation that he was blackmailing Lord Hubert Fitzpatrick as well.

But The Spaniard had had enough. 'Just get the money, Percy. You have three weeks. I'll be in touch. Now fuck off, you're ruining my lunch.'

1975

The trouble in the Midlands had come to an end. The police had hauled close to forty men down the nick through numerous raids on houses and business premises. The two biggest scalps were Taffy Morgan and Vince Connelly. For some reason, King Arthur had escaped the authorities' tightening noose. He wasn't even in hiding, but still continued to run the legitimate side of his business. He had spent four hours down the cop shop being interviewed, but was soon released without charge when his silky-tongued, immaculately dressed, overpaid solicitor turned up. The police had marked King Arthur's card, but they knew that to land this big fish they would have to be far more patient and diligent. He had far too many senior police in his pocket, any officer compiling evidence against this slippery devil would have to have a case more watertight than a swan's bottom.

In the meantime, King Arthur had been doing some diligent investigating himself. Never one to jump in feet first, making snap decisions before all the facts were laid out before him like his son. He had never been completely convinced that the Morgan brothers were responsible for the hold-up of his bookmaker shops. It just didn't make sense to him. The two families had divided up the racecourses and bookies between them. They both earned a bloody good wedge, and relations between them, while not exactly lovey-dovey, were at least respectful and amicable, albeit at arm's length. If they had wanted to muscle in on King Arthur's share, surely they would have started with the course bookies, not just strolled into one of his shops and start shooting up the place demanding money. It was far more likely to be the work of a stranger, an opportunist, or just a plain madman.

Indeed, it did turn out to be a madman, a psychopath named Shotgun Charlie, according to an insider King Arthur had in the Met Police. And this Shotgun Charlie was a known associate of a certain London thug called The Spaniard. At this point in time, King Arthur had not been aware of his son Vince's ambitions to get a foot in the door of the Soho scene, and had thus never heard of this Spaniard before. His only interest was in the bastard that popped his nephew with a shotgun, and was therefore responsible for all this mayhem that had followed. He decided to send his two best hatchet men down to London to find this arsehole and bring him back to the Midlands for a cosy little chat, or failing that, just put a bullet in the back of his head.

'Is that you, Peggy?' called Harry as he heard a noise coming from the club cellar. He glanced at his watch. It was still only 9.30am and Peggy normally didn't make an appearance till 10.30. Harry, on the other hand, was an early bird, a creature of habit. He would arrive and unlock the club at 8.30am, carry the post up to the office, check the safe and last night's takings, fill the kettle, then pop next door to Giovanni's to pick up his usual sausage and mustard sandwich for breakfast. He was just returning from Giovanni's, and on his way into the kitchen to make a cup of tea, when he heard the creak from the cellar. He grabbed the torch from behind the bar and reached for the door handle to the cellar staircase. Just as he did, the door flew open outwards, catching Harry full in the face. He hit the floor, closely followed by the torch in one hand and his sausage sandwich in the other. A huge thickset man stood looking down at Harry spread-eagled on the floor. His ample frame filling the total door frame.

'Yow alright, old man? Sorry 'bout your sarnie there.' The Brummie accent was clear. Harry had a flashback to a conversation he'd had with Pete the Pig, about how one of the fella's in Camelot bookies had been the size of King Kong. No prizes for guessing this was the same ape, which meant that King Arthur had at last put two and two together and got four instead of two – two Morgan Brothers.

'Let me help yow up, old man,' said the ape, as he lifted Harry up by his jacket lapels. Once Harry's feet were literally a foot off the ground, the ape dropped him backwards and down again with heavy force. Harry's head hit a table on the way down, causing a wide gash, and a lot of blood.

Another man then appeared, coming down the stairs leading to the office. Standing on Harry's hand, he casually crouched down so he was closer to Harry's ear.

'My name is Felix, and I see you've already met my associate Brutus. We just paid a visit to a Mr Shotgun Charlie and were very sad to hear of his recent demise. But Mrs Shotgun Charlie – not a particularly attractive woman to say the least, but nevertheless very helpful – seems to think that his death might be the work of a Mr Hammer aka a Mr Spaniard, and we think you know where we might find this Spanish chappy.'

Harry's head was throbbing, and the pain shooting up his arm from the weight of Felix standing on his hand was excruciating. 'Go fuck yourselves,' he managed to splutter out.

'Did you hear that, Brutus? The old fucker has balls of steel.' Felix then leant forward, grabbed Harry's face with his hand spread across Harry's mouth and nose, lifted up Harry's head and then smashed it back down on the tiled floor. Harry's vision blurred and he started to lose consciousness, claret oozing from his skull.

'Come on, Brutus,' said Felix. 'Let's leave the old bastard alone. He ain't going to tell us nothing. Let's try out this sex joint – Pinky's round the corner, maybe Mr Spanish will be there.'

'Guess your right,' replied Brutus, purposely stepping on Harry's genitals, instead of walking around him.

2005

Pepe woke from a deep sleep. It was ten past five in the morning and the phone was ringing continuously. He made it out of bed and to the receiver in the lounge just in time, the caller about to give up. At any other time he probably would have let it continue to ring, just rolling over to resume his slumber. But this was not any other time. This was far from any normal average time in his life. Maggie had felt a little stronger and been released from the hospital a few days before, the demand for beds evidently outweighing her need to be closely cared for. But once out, she had gone dramatically downhill. They had admitted her again two days ago, and yesterday the doctor had told Pepe that the cancer had spread. But spread was a very inadequate term. The reality was it had invaded, infiltrated and ravaged. What started as small-cell lung carcinoma, had metastasized in the liver, the bones and finally the brain. It was only a matter of time, a very short matter of time, warned the doctor.

The voice at the end of the line was calm, almost soothing, had it not been for the underlying urgency. They felt he should go to the hospital straightaway, the end was close.

When he got to the hospital Maggie had been moved. She was now in her own private little room. She no longer had numerous tubes sprouting out of her hands and arms, connected to various drips and machines. Just one now remained, registering what little life was left in this once happy, funny, loving, and beautiful body.

Pepe sat next to his mum and slipped her hand in his. The room was silent apart from the heavy rasping short breaths as Maggie's airways fought for oxygen. The rest of the hospital was just waking up, the nightshift finishing their paperwork, the dayshift arriving. The corridors were beginning to buzz, the kitchens firing into action, the car park filling, but none of that mattered in this little room. Neither of the occupants were aware of the activities beyond the door, their thoughts far, far away. Pepe spoke to Maggie, unable to tell if his message was getting through. Her face, her body, not registering anything. It was the same message over and over again – I love you, mum, I love you so much.

Thirty-five minutes passed. It was the longest thirty-five minutes ever to Pepe in the agony of watching and waiting. And yet it turned out to be the shortest thirty-five minutes, because it was the remaining time he would ever share with his mother. Her breathing stumbled, her head lifted very slightly from the pillow as she started choking.

Pepe let out an anguished cry, 'No! Please...'

Maggie's head dropped back down again and the breathing resumed. But it had taken on a distressing loud grating noise. A coarser breathing, that struggled in vain to get air into her liquid-filled lungs. Pepe tightened the grip on his mum's hand, the tears rolling uncontrollably down his cheeks. The breaths became shorter and louder. And then Maggie opened her eyes.

'Mum, mum,' Pepe called out.

Maggie's eyes appeared to look slowly around the room until they settled on her distraught boy. She remained staring at him for just a couple of seconds, but it was long enough for Pepe to know that she had seen him there, that she would know he had been with

132

her at the end, and that he loved her more than anything. Her eyes then closed forever.

It was another hour before Pepe could leave the room. The nurse had been in once, but he asked her if he could just sit a bit longer on his own with Maggie. He knew this would be the very last time he would be able to look at her, and he wasn't quite ready to say goodbye just yet. Eventually, the nurse came back again and told him there was some tea waiting for him in another room and someone to see him. She showed him into a small waiting room down the end of the corridor. Inside were ten chairs backed against the walls, surrounding a small coffee table with a tray of tea and digestives on it. Next to the tray was a folder entitled 'A Useful Guide – Following the death of a family member'. And pacing round the table like a confined animal in a cage was Samir. They held each other until both had managed to staunch the flow of their own separate tears.

Then Pepe said, 'I want to find Ignacio.'

1975

'Alright, alright, I'm coming.'

The banging on the front door increased in volume and repetition. The Spaniard came down the stairs pulling on a shirt. 'OK, OK! Hold your bloody horses.' He swung open the front door to find a very out-of-breath Pete the Pig sweating profusely.

'What is it? What's the matter?' The Spaniard asked impatiently.

'It's Harry, boss, he's been done over. Peggy found him, she's in a right old state.'

'Where are they?'

'They took Harry to St Thomas' Hospital.'

'Right, let's go,' shouted The Spaniard.

'There's more, boss. Two heavies were in Pinky's looking for you. Big bastards, they were seen leaving Bohemia and walking round to Pinky's. They roughed him up a bit too, but he's OK. He told them you usually pop in around lunchtime. They are probably still in Soho somewhere looking for you.'

'OK – change of plan, let's find them first.'

'Shit! How did I know you would say that, boss?' muttered Pete the Pig, now sweating even more.

'Just start the fucking car, I'll be there in a sec.' The Spaniard then went back into the flat and lifted two old broken floorboards in the understairs cupboard, and pulled out a heavy metal object wrapped in a white cloth. He reached back under the floorboards and scooped up a box of cartridges. Then he removed the white cloth and shoved the Luger P08 pistol in his trouser waistband.

Felix and Brutus were congratulating themselves on their morning's work in the Swiss Tavern, awaiting the arrival of The Spaniard at Pinky's up the street.

Little did they know, The Spaniard was hurtling straight for them at a million miles an hour. One of Pinky's girls had seen them go in the pub and had told The Spaniard when he had pulled up outside. Pinky had also spoken to a distraught Peggy on the phone at the hospital. She told him that Harry had had a heart attack on the way to the hospital and had passed away in the ambulance. The Spaniard was now a volcano about to erupt. Pete the Pig, still one step behind, and petrified, was struggling to keep up. The Spaniard stopped at the corner of Old Compton Street and turned back. 'Listen, Pete, I don't need you on this one.'

Pete the Pig wanted to argue, he wanted to prove to The Spaniard that he wasn't afraid, that he was willing to stand side by side with him and face Harry's assailants, but his nerve was caving in. While he was no coward, and maybe not the sharpest knife in the drawer, he was clever enough to realise that The Spaniard was going to take this to the edge, and anybody in the near vicinity was likely to end up going over. 'But, boss,' he urged, in nothing more than a whisper, the relief on his face blatant.

The Spaniard spoke quickly. 'Get the motor and park it on Romilly Street, out back of the Swiss Tavern. Get out of the car, but leave the engine running. Quick as you can, go now.' Before Pete the Pig could answer, The Spaniard had left the corner and was marching towards the pub.

There were no words, no warnings, no mercy given. The first bullet slammed into the side of Brutus's skull. He stumbled forward, his dead weight almost knocking over Felix. The Spaniard moved in closer, striding through the empty bar. It was a Sunday morning, the bar had only been open fifteen minutes and, apart from Felix and Brutus, the only other customer was Olive, an old pensioner well known in Soho. The Spaniard advanced on Felix, who had escaped the falling body of Brutus and headed towards the Gents', fumbling for his own pistol in his inside jacket pocket. He had just managed to retrieve and cock the Webley revolver when The Spaniard threw open the toilet door and fired two bullets at close range into his chest. Before Felix had even hit the floor The Spaniard was sprinting down the passage between the bar and the kitchen, out over the backyard wall and into the driver's seat of the waiting Jensen Interceptor.

2005

Three weeks had passed since Percival had met Ignacio in the Black Jack. Ignacio had indeed contacted Percival demanding his loot, but Percival had managed to convince him that he needed more time. There was too much paperwork and other factors involved in raising that sum so quickly. It may have been that Ignacio believed him, but more likely it was the news that a new biography was about to hit the bookstalls that softened Ignacio, albeit only very slightly, but enough to buy Percival more time.

The newly published biography was based on the life of Lord Hubert Fitzpatrick. Whilst this event in itself did not have any effect on Ignacio, it was a story being leaked in one of the daily papers that had momentarily distracted him. The paper said that there were certain allegations being made from an undisclosed source, that at the very least would tarnish the reputation of the formidable and illustrious Lord Fitzpatrick. Only one such allegation had been reported thus far, and that was that Dirty Bertie had coerced the judge in a murder trial against The Spaniard thirty years ago. But the author of the article had promised there were more secrets to follow.

Ignacio shook his head in disgust. There had been so much recent publicity surrounding the long-awaited biography of such a prominent lord and Queen's cousin. Clearly the newspaper was keen to jump on the bandwagon and had got some scummy reporter to snoop around and come up with all this shit just to increase newspaper sales.

Or at least this was what Ignacio thought. However, there was one man who knew different. One man who had been tipping the newspaper reporter off.

Percival Davenport smudged the last speck of illicit white powder from his nose and chuckled to himself. The slimy news hack had gobbled up every sordid tale Percy spilt out about Lord Hubert Fitzpatrick, regardless of how true any of it was. His aim to publicly place M'Lord in cahoots with The Spaniard was now achieved. This would hopefully result in Fitzpatrick having even more reason to want Ignacio Perez removed from society. It was all going nicely to plan. Percival was looking forward to his luncheon date at White's, the private gentlemen's club on St James's Street with his host Lord Fitzpatrick. He knew Fitzpatrick had strong ties with the intelligence service. Was it possible he could arrange to have someone rubbed out? Obviously, Percival would have to tread carefully, he didn't want to get his own hands dirty. No, far from it, it should be Fitzpatrick's idea. Percival just needed to sow the seed without implicating himself. Fitzpatrick did not need to know about Percival's own history with The Spaniard. Instead he needed to let Fitzpatrick think that various evidence had been presented to him by an unknown source, possibly the same source that was talking to the newspapers. And they were linking Fitzpatrick with The Spaniard, and several underage girls. Furthermore, it was believed that The Spaniard held in his possession damning photos which he might himself sell to the newspapers. This was, of course, just according to Percival's imaginative plot, as he still had no real confirmation whether The Spaniard did possess such photos. However he was spot on, The Spaniard certainly did have old photos of M'Lord, from back in the seventies, featuring him in both compromising, and rather athletic, positions. But in all this time, The Spaniard had never actually threatened Fitzpatrick with their publication.

Yes, it should be a very interesting lunch. They had met each other several times over the last ten years during Percival's meteoric rise on the political stage. But fortunately for Percival, Fitzpatrick had never recognised him as the young man he'd once bumped into in Club Bohemia thirty years ago. But then, why should he remember some young man sitting quietly in the corner with two rentboys, while he sat with a bevy of young beauties, sipping champagne, laughing, dancing, and generally being the life and soul of the party. Of course, back then in those days Lord Fitzpatrick was also a much younger man, possibly ten years older than Percival, but still able to enjoy his fortunate birth right without the hindrance of today's tabloids and paparazzi.

But then came the eighties with Diana mania, followed closely by the slow meltdown of the royal family. The cracks started to appear, the British public became even more obsessed with the royals, and now the upper classes too, especially their scandalous behaviour. People like M'Lord suddenly had to be far more careful, far more discreet, lest they get caught with their trousers down. It was at this time that Lord Fitzpatrick stopped frequenting clubs like the Bohemia, and definitely distanced himself from people like The Spaniard, which was much easier said than done when it came to Ignacio. The Spaniard had invested a lot of time and money in hooking this big prize, and hung on to him like a pit-bull.

Ever since The Spaniard's empire had started to crumble after that messy business during the eighties in Malaga, resulting in the death of Maltese Tony, Lord Fitzpatrick had occasionally helped him financially. Ignacio was sensible, he never overplayed his hand, and there was never any mention of blackmail. There was no need, both men knew the other's position far too well. They always kept it very friendly and respectful, like a bank manager granting a small loan. A loan that both parties knew would never ever be repaid. As long as it didn't occur any more than annually, and for just a few thousand each time, M'Lord had conceded to it without causing a fuss, however much he resented it inside. Ignacio was wise enough to see this, and was content not to bite the hand that feeds.

1975

It was a busy week for the justice courts in England. The Victoria Law Courts in Birmingham were trying the case of Vincent Brendan Connelly for the murder of Rhys Owen Morgan at Hereford racecourse. And London's Old Bailey was featuring Ignacio Romero Perez aka The Spaniard, on trial for the murder of Felix McNamara and Tracy O'Shea aka Brutus, in the Swiss Tavern, Soho.

'Cor, fuck me, no wonder he changed his name to Brutus,' chuckled Pete the Pig as he read the morning paper. 'Tracy? It's a bloody girl's name, isn't it? How many fella's do you know called Tracy?' he asked Tel-Boy, who was sitting opposite him in the cafe along Wardour Street.

'I'd like to have seen you call him Tracy,' commented Tel-Boy, in between large mouthfuls of beans, bangers, and mash.

'Yeah, well, I won't need to any more now, will I? Not now he's brown bread.' The words lingered in the air between them. For a moment they both sat in silence, lost in their own thoughts about the events of that bloody and deadly day.

'I don't mind telling you I'm pleased I wasn't in that pub when the boss let them have it. I mean, it's all very well handing out a few slaps, a bit of fisty-cuffs never hurt anybody, but to just walk in there and shoot them at point-blank range, well that's just… just bloody insane. He'll go down for life, they'll throw the bloody book at him, you mark my words.'

Tel-Boy looked up from his beans and studied Pete the Pig for a moment. 'I wouldn't be so certain, if I were you. I wouldn't write the boss off just yet, he's far too smart, and that barrister he's got – Loophole Sinclair, he could get the bloody Ripper off.'

Pete the Pig let out a snort of derision. 'I think it will take more than a fuckin' loophole to get him off cold-blooded murder, mate! Honestly, he may be Loophole Sinclair but he ain't Ali fucking Bongo.'

'Mock all you like,' said Tel-Boy, shaking his head. 'But don't forget the boss has got some serious movers in his pocket. He knows some very influential people. And what's more, he knows their dirty little secrets. I'm sure he'll be calling in a few favours.'

'Yeah, that's all very well, but what about witnesses,' Pete the Pig asked smugly.

'What witnesses? asked Tel-boy

'You mean old Olive? Everybody knows she's away with the fairies, they'll never get anything sensible out of her, she's *radio rental*, mate.'

'Well, what about the barman?' asked Pete the Pig, determined not to concede.

'At the time of the shooting he wasn't even in the bar, he was out the back changing the barrels or something,' replied Tel-Boy. 'Anyway, I'm sure he knows who the boss is, they all do around here. He would be a very brave fucker if he stood up and gave evidence against The Spaniard.'

Pete the Pig sat back and shook his head. 'Well, I'm still not so sure. I tell you what, if he walks away from this I'll eat my hat,' he scoffed.

Tel-Boy grinned. 'It's about the only thing left you haven't fuckin' eaten!'

Just as Tel-Boy said, The Spaniard was indeed looking for favours, and top of his list was Lord Fitzpatrick. Not only was he a regular four-ball golfing partner of the presiding judge, but coincidently he was godfather to one of the young female jurors. The police had still not found the weapon, and as yet nothing or nobody had put The Spaniard at the murder scene. The prosecutor's case was precariously resting mainly on police hearsay, and Loophole Sinclair was making them look totally inept.

In complete contrast, the case against Vincent Brendan Connelly was looking extremely damning, the evidence against him very convincing. There were three witnesses willing to identify Vince as the one that inflicted multiple stab wounds to Rhys Morgan. Also the knife used had been recovered by the police and was smothered in Vince's fingerprints. The judge was about to hand out a life sentence with a recommendation that a minimum of thirty years be served. It would be a very long time before Vince Connelly breathed the air of a free man again.

'Have you seen Peggy recently?' Pete the Pig asked Tel-Boy.

'Nah, not since last Friday. I think she's gone down Southend to stay with her daughter Shirley. Why?'

'Mmm… nothing really,' said Pete the Pig, lost in thought again. 'Well it's just… well, I just don't understand how bad she took old Harry's death. She was really cut-up about it, and even now, three months later, she still keeps breaking down.'

Tel-Boy gave him a curious stare. 'You do know they were married for over forty years, don't you? What do you expect?'

'Married? What do you mean married? They bloody hated each other. They were always arguing. Old Peg never had one good word to say about him.'

'That was just their way,' said Tel-Boy. 'I guess after forty-odd years you're so used to each other, it's like water off a duck's back. A lot of it was just show, they never actually upset each other.'

'I don't believe it,' exclaimed Pete the Pig. 'Are you sure they were married?'

'Of course I am. You think I would just make that up to humour you? Don't you remember a couple of years ago the boss giving them a load of *sausage and mash* to spend on a holiday? And they went off to Benidorm for a week.'

'Yeah, vaguely,' answered Pete the Pig. 'But I didn't know they was abroad, and I certainly didn't know they were going on holiday with each other.'

Tel-Boy let out a long sigh. 'It was their fuckin' fortieth anniversary, you great pillock. Of course they were going together. Fuck me! You don't know Jack Squat, do you?'

Pete the Pig's ample cheeks blushed an embarrassed shade of purple, as it all started to make sense to him. 'You know, I wondered why they both came back the colour of nig-nogs.'

'Oh, hallelujah!' shouted out Tel-Boy. 'Well done, Sparky! You know, sometimes I'm not sure your elevator goes all the way to the penthouse,' he said, shaking his head in amusement.

'You what? What's a fuckin' elevator got to do with it?' asked Pete the Pig.

'Nothing, let's just drop it, shall we? Go and pay the bill,' Tel-Boy said, totally exhausted.

When he returned from the cashier, Tel-Boy noticed that Pete the Pig had suddenly got a very worried look on his face. 'Now what's the matter?' he asked.

'With Prince Vince about to go down for a thirty stretch, and The Spaniard possibly not around any more, do you think King Arthur will come looking for us?'

It was at times like this that Tel-Boy saw the vulnerable little boy hiding in Pete's bountiful frame, and couldn't help but feel protective over him. 'Don't worry, nobody will be coming after you. The boss told me he made contact with King Arthur and they had quite a little heart to heart. The boss put him right about Vince's little antics down here, trying to squeeze protection money from the club. Evidently, the old man didn't have a clue, and wasn't too impressed by his son's behaviour. He conceded with the boss that Shotgun Charlie's early demise squared it as far as his nephew being blasted full of lead was concerned.'

'What about the boss plugging Felix and Brutus?' asked Pete the Pig.

'Well, as the boss said to King Arthur – If you send a couple of troublemakers looking for me, then that's exactly what they're gonna get… big trouble. If Felix and Brutus hadn't picked on poor old Harry, then the boss would have sent them packing with just a light bruising and a loss of pride, but they went too far. Harry was like a stepdad to the boss.'

'And King Arthur just accepted all this?' Pete the Pig asked doubtfully.

'Well… I'm not so sure I would have put it quite like that. Let's just say he agreed there had been enough grief. There was too much police attention, and he was getting too old for all this bloodshed. They agreed that the matter would end now between them. But King Arthur did make one last statement. He said that while there would be no more retaliation from him or any of

145

his men, he could not speak for his son. Knowing his son as well as he does, he thought it unlikely that Vince would ever drop the matter. Particularly as whenever he looks in the mirror, he has a permanent reminder of The Spaniard, due to the fact that the top of his left ear is missing. And should he eventually get released from prison, he will be sure to come looking for retribution.'

PART TWO

2005

A Letter

It had been surprisingly easier to track down Ignacio than Pepe had initially anticipated. Granted he had a lucky break, when he met up again with his Aunt Pru after several years, at Maggie's funeral. She was the spiteful sister that Maggie had never got on with. She had been unusually forthcoming when Pepe questioned her after everyone else had left. Not that Aunt Pru had ever been one to keep her thoughts and opinions to herself, particularly when it came to her younger sister Maggie. However, in the past, she was always quite tight-lipped around Pepe if ever the subject of his childhood or father arose. But now, marinating in a mixture of grief and dry sherry, she was letting it all wash out. Had she been aware of Pepe's real motive — that he was actively trying to find his father, then she might well have kept her mouth shut, but Pepe had caught her off-guard and vulnerable. Now that Maggie was no longer there to defend herself, Pru had lost all her fight. All that petty disapproval and resentfulness had now been replaced by remorse. Pepe could have asked her anything, and Aunt Pru would have duly answered with unguarded honesty. Now she needed to exorcise all that ill-feeling she had harboured against Maggie over the years. She was thankful to be given the opportunity to admit that maybe she hadn't always been right, that deep down she had cared very much, and had always wished the relationship between them had been less volatile. Maggie was her sister, and as such, she had always loved her.

Aunt Pru was a true spinster, living all her life at the same address in Willesden Green with her two cats – Boudicca and Aphrodite. The small two-bedroomed terrace had been where she and Maggie had grown up with their parents, until they were killed in a tragic car accident when Maggie had just turned fourteen. Prunella was ten years Maggie's senior, and had therefore been left in charge of looking after her as a guardian. Because of the age gap, and her own very strict upbringing, she had a very different view on how a teenage girl should behave. Having grown up in the austere fifties and not the swinging sixties like Maggie, her ideals were rather more prim and proper. But it was a time of rock 'n' roll and rebellion, and Maggie embraced both as a troubled teen becoming a young lady. This caused bitter feuds between the two of them, right up until Maggie moved out at twenty and went to live with Ignacio. Unfortunately, instead of the quarrels ending, this caused an even bigger rift between them because of Prunella's disapproval and outright animosity towards Ignacio.

Now, while chatting to Aunt Pru, Pepe learnt that around five years ago, Ignacio had actually tried to find the whereabouts of Maggie. Knowing it was a safe bet that Prunella would still be living at the same address, he had sent a card there addressed to Maggie, in the hope that Prunella would pass it on to her. He obviously had no idea where Maggie was, or with whom, but it was highly likely that Prunella would. He also knew that nosy Pru was bound to open the card and, seeing who it was from, probably bin it immediately. After all, she had actively tried to discourage the relationship between Maggie and Ignacio all those years ago. Plus with everything that had been written about him in the press, he was certain her repulsion towards him would only have intensified over the last twenty-five years. So he had written a covering note appealing to her better nature, saying that not only did he want to get in touch with Maggie, but also he wanted to hear some news about their son. To add to the emotional blackmail, he had also enclosed a cheque made payable to Pepe for five thousand pounds. This understandably came as quite a shock to Pepe when Aunt Pru mentioned this. Unsurprisingly, however, Prunella had sent the cheque back to Ignacio telling him that neither Maggie nor Pepe needed his dirty money, and they certainly would not welcome any contact from him now, or indeed ever.

Unwittingly, Aunt Pru then gave away Ignacio's address, when she smugly announced to Pepe, 'He's come to nothing just like I always said, living in some sheltered housing in Peckham. Should be in a padded cell in Broadmoor, if you ask me. Is there no real justice in this world? Locked up and the key thrown away for good. He's a wrong'un, that one, always was, but your mother would never have it. Even after she left him, I would find her weeping for him... I suppose we should be grateful that one good thing came out of it all – they had you. At least you turned out to be a decent boy, a little wild at times, but you've got some sense. You'll make a fine husband and father one day, although you're leaving it a bit too late in my opinion.'

Pepe felt himself biting his tongue. Nobody had ever been brave enough to tell Aunt Pru that Pepe was gay. And however tempted Pepe was to tell her right now – that he liked nothing better than a bit of man-on-man action, with lots of rimming thrown in for good measure – he decided today of all days was probably not the right time. She'd had to cope with enough emotional upset watching her younger sister be buried. She would probably throw herself on top of the coffin if she found out her nephew was a raving nancy boy.

After his informative chat with Aunt Pru, and with the help of the internet, a couple of phone calls later, Pepe had a full address for Ignacio Perez scrawled on his Ant & Dec calendar. It turned out there were only five sheltered housing schemes in Peckham, and Pepe had got lucky on his second call. Now all he needed to do was write a letter. A letter to the father who he last saw thirty years ago when he was only three years old. And as hard as he tried, he did not have one memory of him from that time. At the outset, Pepe had thought that finding him would be the hard part, and making contact with him a piece of piss. But now, perched at the table facing a blank writing pad, with pen poised in hand, it seemed the other way around. Pepe struggled to come up with the words he needed for a man he knew so little of, with the exception of having read about several suspected murders during a long career as a hardened criminal.

A Luncheon

Although Percival Davenport was a member of White's gentlemen's club, he rarely passed through its imposing dark wood doors. As the unofficial headquarters of the Tory party any self-respecting, high-ranking Conservative politician should have hurdled the stiff membership criteria, and got himself accepted. But it was exactly these strict rules, old-fashioned values, and general snobbishness that put Percival off. When he was young he would have done anything to be embraced into the rich tobacco-smelling leather upholstery, and private panelled rooms. He had been desperate to get the attention of, and to impress the country's old influential nobility. He had actively crept, crawled and cajoled until he received an invitation with the right distinguished names to sponsor his membership. But now he had little time for all that old-boy nonsense. He saw himself as a man of the future, a visionary. He had already accumulated the support and backing of the country's high-powered money men and captains of industry. He had no further need of the fading aristocracy and their tired old etiquette.

Once inside the club, he wasn't surprised to see very little had changed since he had last dined there nearly five years previously. However, he was slightly startled to see that Lord Hubert Fitzpatrick now had the honour and privilege of occupying the table in the famous bow window, a place reserved for only the most respected members. It is said that back in 1816, William Arden, 2nd Baron Alanley, use to occupy this esteemed seat, and it was here that he wagered a friend three thousand pounds on which of two raindrops running down the window pane would reach the bottom first. It was no shock with spending habits like this in the early 1800s, that Baron Alanley a few years later had to sell off his vast family estates.

Bertie Fitzpatrick greeted Percival warmly. 'My dear chap, it must be over a year since we last crossed paths. I've been racking my simple old brain trying to think exactly when it was.'

'I believe it was during the Queen's golden jubilee in 2002,' Percival reminded him. 'Didn't we bump into each other at the Party at the Palace? The rock concert held in the gardens.'

'Good god, man, was it really that long ago? Three years? I vaguely recollect it,' Dirty Bertie said, shaking his silver-haired head.

'I'm surprised you don't remember making a complete sexual menace of yourself backstage with Atomic Kitten and S Club 7' thought Percival, but decided not to bring that up.

Their lunch together was indeed a very affable affair. That is, until Percival mentioned the name Ignacio Perez. At that point Lord Bertie dropped his delicate dessert spoon directly into the middle of his baked orange soufflé, causing it to rapidly deflate, and sending the Grand Marnier and kumquat marmalade splattering into his glass of Sauternes.

'How on earth do you know that scoundrel?' he asked.

Percival explained that a journalist contact of his, who he kept on side for obvious advantages, had mentioned in passing that he had been offered incriminating evidence of M'Lord with under-aged girls by a certain Ignacio Perez back in the 70s. As yet the newspaper involved had not agreed on a price with the source, and the journalist was not in receipt of such evidence, but it was surely only a matter of time before an editor signed a large cheque.

This news clearly had quite an effect on Dirty Bertie as he pushed his uneaten very sorry-looking soufflé aside and ordered a large Hennessey cognac. By the time he had drunk his third cognac, Percival had left him in no doubt that Ignacio was about to seize the day. With M'Lord's memoirs shortly to be published, it would be impeccable timing to make public any damaging sleaze. The price a newspaper would normally pay dramatically increasing with all the current hype and interest. Ignacio was about to sell M'Lord down the river to the highest bidder, and it would therefore be in Bertie's best interests to remove this distasteful dirt from his fingernails.

'Are you suggesting what I think you are?' asked Bertie, with a certain amount of disdain.

'I'm not suggesting anything,' Percival replied with mutual haughtiness. 'What I'm saying is that society should be protected from repugnant criminals like Ignacio Perez. A known murderer and extortionist, wandering freely through the fair streets of London, spreading his vile and heinous behaviour. And not just in the gutters and slums where he belongs, but even attacking the upper echelons of our nation. Good honest decent people like yourself, who have served this great country with honour and distinction.'

This seemed to go down very well with M'Lord, who puffed out his chest and cleared his throat, 'Quite right, quite right, old boy.'

But Percival wasn't about to let go now. His fish may have been safely hooked, but he still wanted to reel it in and leave it no chance of wriggling free. 'It's a crying shame that the courts of justice have been unable to secure a proper conviction against this scum. The law has done all it can to detain this animal, but others have conspired to halt the wheels of justice.' As he said this, Percival purposely looked away to save M'Lord being caught blushing red. The words alone were sufficient to put M'Lord so ill at ease, that right now he could have murdered The Spaniard with his own bare hands for placing him in this sickening position.

He had naturally been horrified when, thirty years ago, The Spaniard had asked him to speak to the judge in his murder case against Felix McNamara and Tracy O'Shea. He had tried everything to convince The Spaniard that he simply could not ask his honourable friend – Justice James to adopt a sympathetic view of the case against The Spaniard and turn hostile towards the police's lack of evidence. But this had fallen on deaf ears, and The Spaniard had made it quite clear, in no uncertain terms, that he expected M'Lord to do the sensible thing if he knew what was good for him! Thus Dirty Bertie had relented and put in a good word for The Spaniard, as well as sweetening up the old judge by getting him on the guest list for a shooting weekend at Balmoral.

M'Lord tried to settle himself as Percival continued, 'I think we have a duty here as public servants. We have a duty to banish men like this once and for all. For the common good of the country.'

M'Lord was now physically agitated and, Percival hoped, sufficiently motivated. There were beads of sweat appearing on his face, and a twitch developing in the left corner of his mouth, as he rapped his fingers on the table. 'Yes, yes, I see your point. Something should be done,' M'Lord concurred.

When Percival finally stepped out of White's smiling slyly to himself, it was into the deluge that was pouring over London. He had forgotten his umbrella, but nothing could dampen his high spirits, and he decided to continue walking rather than hail a taxi. His mind carefully picked over the conversation he had just had with Fitzpatrick, and all the possible outcomes. He couldn't be certain Fitzpatrick would spring into action. It seemed likely, but there were no guarantees the old fool would follow up. He certainly had the contacts to erase someone. During the Thatcher years he had been a close adviser to MI6 in relation to the IRA. It had been the IRA's aggression and loathing towards Thatcher and her cabinet, after her refusal to meet their demands during the 1980/81 prison hunger strikes, that culminated in the bombing of the Brighton Grand Hotel. It was around this time that Fitzpatrick had played an active role in the intelligence service, sparking rumours that he had worked as an agent himself in his younger days.

By the time Percival had reached the end of Birdcage Walk he was soaked, but enraptured. He had decided that he had no choice but to take out a little insurance policy himself, on the off-chance that M'Lord failed to act. He would have to engage the services of someone to take care of The Spaniard, should M'Lord not have the balls to do so. The thought of this filled him with an equal measure of fear and elation.

A Black Widow

The morning post brought two very big surprises for Ignacio. The first was the daily newspaper with a headline on page six: *'Morgan Mob Murderer released from Belmarsh'*. The second was a letter claiming to be from his son. He put the letter down after reading it through twice. He then flicked on the kettle and made himself his fourth mug of tea of the morning and picked up the newspaper again.

'Vincent Connelly, who in 1975 was the man responsible for leaving gang leader Gareth Morgan hospitalised in a coma for six weeks and the fatal stabbing of Gareth Morgan's nephew Rhys Morgan, walked free from Belmarsh prison yesterday after serving thirty years of a life sentence.'

Ignacio folded the paper neatly into four, then deposited it into the flip-top rubbish bin. He then made himself two pieces toast with plum jam, took another big slurp of tea, and settled down to read Pepe's letter for the third time.

In another kitchen, sixteen miles across London, was a cloying smell of cat litter and stew. It was almost impossible to see out of the window overlooking what used to be a back garden. Not because it was misted up from the steam of the big pan of boiling beef cubes, but because of the build-up of twenty years of filth and grime. This was possibly a blessing, as it screened the plethora of household crap that was piled high in the yard beyond - an outstanding collection of broken washing machines, televisions, bikes, sodden mattresses and busted sofas, to name but a few. Inside, the walls had once been decorated in a bright yellow, orange, and brown floral paper, which now curled unenthusiastically away from the walls, in a desperate bid to detach itself completely and make a run for it. The ancient worktop and splashback tiles were in a clashing avocado colour, but some eager DIYer had recently made an effort to renew the three rows of tiles in gleaming white. Unfortunately they had obviously run out of tiles before completing the task, so there was now a mix of white and avocado tiles at two ends of the kitchen. However, to overcome this eyesore, and in an effort to harmonise the look, someone had ingeniously used avocado-coloured grout. The cupboard doors were a fake dark-wood effect, most of which hung limply from their hinges, defying gravity, and totally unwilling to be closed properly any more. Covering all these walls, worktops and cupboards was a tenacious film of grease. And languishing in the middle of all this decay – the most unpleasant object of all – sat Molly McCray in her dressing gown. Not even the chirpy sounds of Terry Wogan drifting out of the ketchup-splattered radio could cheer up this depressing setting.

The front door opened, and then slammed closed. Molly could hear the crashing and cursing of her younger son forcing his bicycle into the hallway and trying to make room to lean it amongst the other debris.

'Hey, Ma, guess what I've got here?' the big strapping lad called, taking off his Burberry cap, revealing a mop of unkempt ginger hair, similar to his dead father's. He handed her a creased-up yellow post-it note across the kitchen table. She put down her twenty-third cigarette of the morning and put on her glasses.

'It's an address,' he said excitedly.

'Well, yes, I can see that, son. But why all the commotion? Who's it bloody for? Lord fuckin' Lucan?'

'No, Ma. It's for him... the bastard who killed Dad.'

'What?' Molly stared down at the post-it note again. 'You mean this is the address for Ignacio Perez?' she asked cautiously. 'Where did you get it from?'

'Old Jock down the scrapyard. I took me Vauxhall Nova down there first thing this morning. We were just having a natter, turns out his brother lives in the same block as The fuckin' Spaniard. Jock recognised him when he went to see his brother last weekend. Walked straight past the bastard coming out of his front door. I'll go and fuckin' do 'em, Ma.'

'Hang on, hang on, brains. We need to think about this first before you go doing something stupid. Get yer bruvver on the phone, he'll know how best to handle this.'

162

A Reunion

'Morning, Ignacio. Bit early for you, ain't it? I've just this minute opened up,' Wally greeted Ignacio cheerfully as he pushed open the door of the Black Jack pub.

'Alright, Wally. I'm meeting someone this morning, thought I'd get a pint in first.'

'Oh yeah, she nice, is she?' winked Wally.

'Cor, I wish,' laughed Ignacio with him. 'Chance would be a fine thing. I tell you what, Wally, once you get to my age nothing from the waist down works properly. I can't remember the last time I had a good tremble.'

'Me neither, mate,' Wally said, shaking his head.

'Really? Don't your lovely missus give you no nookie?' Ignacio teased him.

'Only when there's nothing decent on TV,' sighed Wally. 'So, who you meeting, if you don't mind me asking?' Even though he and Ignacio had become quite pally over the five years that Ignacio had been frequenting the Black Jack, Wally was still wary of him. He would have a bit of a laugh and a joke with him, but always allowed a respectful amount of privacy. And he never asked too much unless it was volunteered. Wally had recognised Ignacio the very first day he set foot in the pub. He had remembered reading all about The Spaniard in the seventies and eighties – the hardest cold-blooded villain out there. So he had been pretty surprised one day when he looked up from his wife's *Good Housekeeping* magazine and saw the man himself casually leant on the bar, ordering a pack of pork scratchings and a pint. Of course, he never mentioned to Ignacio that he knew who he was, which suited them both. Ignacio never discussed his past, and Wally never questioned him about it.

'Actually, I'm meeting my son,' Ignacio told him.

'Oh… right you are,' Wally replied. It was news to him that Ignacio had a son. He had never mentioned any wife or family before. It was a subject that had never come up between them, and as such, Wally decided not to pry any further.

'Well, if you need me, just give me a shout. I'm going through to bottle up in the other bar. Oh, before I go, there was something I thought I should tell you…' Wally paused.

'Well? What is it?' asked Ignacio.

'Well… erm… I just thought I better let you know… You remember those three lads in here that you had a bit of argy-bargy with?'

Ignacio's black eyes narrowed. 'Yes.'

'Well, they came back in the other afternoon looking for you.'

'Really?' Ignacio's face turned to rigid stone. 'And?'

'Well, I told 'em to sling their hook. Said I'd call the law if they came in again. Sorry, Ignacio, I just thought you should know.'

Ignacio took a long sip on his pint. 'Don't worry, Wally. You did the right thing. It's not worth losing any sleep over.'

'OK, Ignacio,' Wally said, walking through to the other bar. He couldn't help thinking that if he was Ignacio he might be having a few sleepless nights. He had not been totally forthcoming with Ignacio. Before Wally had threatened the lads with the law, they had made some very chilling threats of their own, in particular what they would do the next time they saw Ignacio. Wally was no stranger to trouble himself. He was ex-Army, and fifteen years younger than Ignacio, but still he would be more than a little concerned if it had been him that upset these three bovver boys.

It was an hour later when a tall handsome young man walked in. He had jet-black hair and big chocolate-brown eyes. There could be no mistaking who he was. Ignacio slid off his bar stool and moved forward to greet this familiar stranger.

'Pepe,' he said, as he held out his hand.

'Ignacio?' Pepe inquired back. They shook hands warmly, but were then both hesitant as to what should follow.

'Have a drink?' Ignacio said, nodding at the bar stool next to his.

'Sure, pint of Guinness would be good,' Pepe smiled.

'Wally! Guinness please,' Ignacio called through to the other bar, then turned to face Pepe. He found himself looking in a mirror thirty years ago. He wanted to just sit and stare at his boy. To take him all in, to study every feature, every mannerism, every detail of his character. Desperate to fill in the missing years, to know his son as he should.

'Alright?' Pepe said, nodding at the beaming old man staring intently at him.

'Alright? Alright? I'm more than alright, my son. You have no idea how happy I am right now.'

'Good. Me too,' grinned Pepe.

Pepe couldn't get over how different Ignacio was from the old newspaper cuttings he had kept as a teenager. He had been so big back then, so solid, a strong handsome man. Not that he looked weak or frail now, far from it. He was still a big man, but now he had a slight stoop, the once broad shoulders and barrel chest slightly dropped, the declining bone mass reducing his height. The once thick oiled black hair now thin and peppered with white. The lines on his face telling the story of a life full of trouble and anguish.

They sat looking at each other until Wally had served up the pint of Guinness and retreated back to the other bar, leaving them both in peace.

'How's your mother?' was Ignacio's first question.

Pepe stared down at the floor, the pain rushing back. 'She died three weeks ago.'

When he looked back up at Ignacio he could see tears appear in his eyes. Unbeknown to Pepe, this was only the second time Ignacio had ever cried in his adult life, the first time was also because of Maggie – back when she had taken Pepe and left him all those years ago in Earls Court.

'Oh, son, no. Tell me about it.'

By the time Pepe had finished telling Ignacio about the illness, the treatment, the hospital visits, and eventual passing of Maggie, both of them had wept openly in front of each other. A father–son bond between them had been renewed after thirty long years. By sharing their grief and sadness they had immediately found some common ground, something that brought them instantly back together.

The following hours passed quickly. Both of them had so many questions they wanted to ask, but it was Pepe who talked the most. Ignacio was much keener to hit Pepe with a barrage of questions than to speak about himself. He was desperate to fill in the last thirty years. He wanted to hear all about Maggie and her life, and then everything about Pepe growing up, until now. He briefly touched on his own life during the eighties, how he wound up living in Spain for many years, avoiding the authorities after being suspected of being

166

involved in the £26 million Brink's-Mat bullion robbery from a warehouse in Heathrow in 1983. A total of 6,800 bars of gold were taken, the majority of which had never been recovered. He joked with Pepe how anyone wearing gold in Britain after that was probably wearing Brink's-Mat gold that he had smelted down.

Pepe asked him about the murder of Maltese Tony in Malaga in '86, but Ignacio shrugged that off. 'I won't lie to you, son, I've done my share of bad things, but now's not the time for all that. Let's leave it for another day, yeah? Tell me about your work. You say you've got your own company, I'm proud of you, son.'

They ended up getting fairly pissed together, stumbling out of the Black Jack around 5pm, and then continuing in the curry house up the road till around 8pm. Then Pepe, concerned about Ignacio getting too drunk, decided he should walk him back to his flat.

Ignacio couldn't help laughing. Pepe may have been a reasonable drinker, but he certainly wasn't in Ignacio's league, and it was Ignacio propping up Pepe all the way down the high street, not the other way around. Once home, Ignacio insisted on hailing a taxi for Pepe, and stuffed a couple of tenners in his top pocket.

'Let's do this again, son,' smiled Ignacio.

'You bet, Dad,' grinned Pepe. Then they hugged, they hugged so tight, neither wanting to be the first to let go.

Eventually Ignacio released him. 'Call me next week, you got my number. Now, get in that taxi, you soft chump.'

Pepe slumped in the waiting taxi, little knowing that those would be the last words he would ever hear his father say.

A Grisly Slaying

It was a vicious and unheroic death. A cowardly and merciless attack. A frenzied stabbing assault from behind. Nine fatal strokes. The blade so long and sharp, each time it tore its way through his back it found another vital organ, puncturing his spleen, kidneys and liver. Some would say that it was a bloody and predictable end to such a violent life. There were many who thought he deserved it: good riddance to bad rubbish. But there were also just as many who would privately mourn him. Those who had been seduced by the thrill and excitement of such a dangerous man. Charmed and intrigued by a man that had become a legend in the London underworld. A man that had once run a very successful business empire and had over the years made and lost more money than the average working man would see in a lifetime. He had taken the life of others but had never found real happiness in his own. This was the man that now lay dying alone in the darkness of his own doorway, the blood draining from his body, the life seeping out of him.

A Cremation

Pepe and Samir sat in the anteroom, just off the crematorium chapel. The service was due to take place at 2pm. It was already ten minutes to, and there were only six other people waiting in the room. One was the caretaker/manager of the flats where Ignacio had lived, along with two of his neighbours. The fourth was Wally from the Black Jack pub, and the last two were very obvious CID.

'Not exactly popular, was he?' Samir whispered to Pepe, then instantly regretting it, as he watched Pepe bite down on his lower lip. Just as they were being ushered into the chapel for the service to begin, the outside door opened and in walked a man in his mid fifties, pushing a wheelchair with a very elderly looking lady in it.

They all went into the chapel and sat behind the large rosewood-effect coffin, courtesy of the Co-op. It had been the caretaker/manager from Ignacio's sheltered housing who had arranged the funeral, with the assistance of a solicitor, as Ignacio had died intestate. To their knowledge, there was no will or known relatives at that time. It was only later that Tom, Ignacio's next-door neighbour, mentioned the existence of Pepe. Luckily the morning before he was killed, Ignacio had told Tom about meeting his son after all these years. It had been a couple of weeks since the death, allowing time for a coroner's inquest and post mortem to take place. Pepe had been trying to call his father for the last few days, and was extremely shocked and upset when he received a letter from the solicitor just two days ago informing him of his father's death. The letter continued in a very detached tone. The paperwork may take some time, but the solicitor informed Pepe that he did not see any reason why Ignacio's minimal estate would not be passed on to him. As far as he could ascertain, it amounted to only a few thousand kept in a building society account.

The service was brief, far too brief really. The summation of sixty-five years on earth dispensed with in just six and a half minutes. One minute for each year of life. A brief introduction from the minister, an obscure dreary reading, a hymn – 'Jerusalem', Ignacio's favourite, according to Tom the neighbour, and a short prayer. Of course, the minister could have spoken considerably longer about the life and career of Ignacio Romero Perez. After all, his speech was not kept short due to the lack of details available to him. It was kept short because the minister did not wish to poison the air with an account of an existence so violent it was a miracle he had even lived to the age of sixty-five. Instead, he condensed the majority of Ignacio's adulthood into one sentence: '*It was a life that trod the path of both right and wrong.*' An understatement by any stretch of the imagination, thought Wally, a thought also shared by both Samir and the two CID coppers, who turned and raised their eyebrows at each other. With the prayer done, the curtain closed around the coffin, the service was complete. Pepe was then directed to the side door going out to the garden of remembrance, where he led the fellow mourners behind him.

The two CID coppers, seeing that no one of interest, no faces from the past or possible suspects were about to show up, muttered their condolences to Pepe, and quickly departed. So too, the caretaker/manager and the two neighbours, leaving just Wally and the man with the lady in the wheelchair.

The man extended his hand and introduced himself to Pepe. 'Hi, I'm Terry Shooter, I worked for your dad a long time ago. I'm very sorry for your loss.'

'Thank you for coming,' Pepe said, not quite sure what else to say. 'This is my mate, Sambo ' he nodded at Samir, and Tel-Boy and Samir shook hands.

'You look like your dad,' Tel-Boy smiled at Pepe, and then, leaning down to the ear of the elderly lady in the wheelchair, he spoke in a loud voice, 'He looks just like his father, doesn't he, Peggy?'

She nodded enthusiastically, her little grey head bobbing up and down. She put her hand out towards Pepe. He instinctively accepted it in his, and she tugged him down towards her. 'He was a lovely-looking man, just like you, dear,' she said, still nodding at Pepe, as he bent forward. Then she tugged his arm again, and Pepe, realising she wanted to say much more, crouched down on his haunches in front of her, still holding her hand. He noticed her arm was shaking with the onset of Parkinson's disease. He could see her eyes were filling with water. 'He was a good man, you know. Don't believe everything you hear about him. I know he could be a bit of a wrong'un. He didn't always see eye to eye with people, but he had a good heart. He always looked after me and my Harry. He was very special to us. Him and my Harry really cared for each other, like a father and son, otherwise Ignacio wouldn't have done what he did, would he?' she asked, looking up at Tel-Boy. But Tel-Boy remained silent, not quite overcome with the same sentimental delusions as Peggy.

'I'm so sorry, pet,' Peggy continued. 'It's a shame you didn't get to spend more time with each other, especially when you was growing up, but nobody

171

blamed your mother for that. She did what she thought was best for you. How is she? How is your mother, pet?'

Now the tears started to well up in Pepe's eyes. He hadn't been prepared for this. The death of Ignacio was obviously upsetting enough for him, particularly as he had only just been reunited with his father, but compounded with the fact that he had lost Maggie as well, he found it hard to keep back the tears.

'She died. Just recently,' came Samir to Pepe's rescue. Both Tel-Boy and Peggy stared at Samir in confused shock, allowing Pepe time to compose himself.

Getting off his haunches and standing back up, he wiped his eyes. 'She had lung cancer.'

'Oh fuck,' said Tel-Boy, momentarily forgetting his surroundings, then immediately apologising. 'Oh sorry, I mean... well... sorry, kid.

The four of them were left silent, and it was Wally this time who came to the rescue. 'Look, my pub is not far from here. How about we all go back and have a drink. It's on me, call it a little wake for Ignacio.'

The others all agreed, they certainly all felt like having a bloody good drink. Even Peggy felt a couple of port and lemons wouldn't go amiss. So they hopped into their respective cars and followed Wally back to the Black Jack.

After a couple of drinks and a bit of LIDL lasagne that Wally heated up in the microwave, Tel-Boy said he'd better be getting Peggy back home to her daughter's place in Southend. Peggy would have been quite happy to stay for a third port and lemon, she was already feeling quite tipsy, but Tel-Boy wanted to hit the road. He reluctantly gave Pepe his contact number when Pepe asked for it. Not that he had anything against

Pepe, but, as he told him, he never thought about the old days any more. It had been a long time ago when he worked for his dad, and he had put all that behind him. He stayed within the law now, married with a couple of teenage daughters, running his own reputable security firm. The days of working as muscle on the doors and playing the heavy when necessary were a distant memory. He had come today just to show his respects, and because Peggy had asked him to bring her.

When Pepe asked if he had any idea who could have done this to his father, Tel-Boy changed the subject fast. This wasn't a conversation he wanted to be getting himself into. He had put the past firmly behind him, and intended for it to stay that way. He very politely told Pepe he was very sorry but he wasn't able to fill in any of the blanks about his father.

It was after Tel-Boy and Peggy had left the pub that Wally let slip that Ignacio had recently had a bit of fisty-cuffs with three yobs in the pub. He didn't notice quite how alert Pepe became on hearing this. Wally had prattled on about how the lads had come back again and made threats, without quite realising the enormity of what he was saying. Nor did he sense the agitation rising up in Pepe as he gently probed Wally for more details. But Samir did. Knowing Pepe as well as he did, Samir knew what he was thinking straightaway, and furthermore he could sense the inevitable trouble that would undoubtedly follow.

A Reconnaissance

'Come on, Dorothy, can't you just drop it? Let the police deal with it.'

'Yeah right, the police. What do you think they are going to do about it?' Pepe fired back. 'You saw those two cops at Ignacio's funeral, just a jolly day out for them. Hard-nosed detectives? More like the Chuckle Brothers, if you ask me. You heard Wally in the pub, he said they hadn't even interviewed him, yet Ignacio drank in there every single day. Do you not think they should be going over his regular activities and who he came into contact with? Surely his local boozer would be a good source of info? They're not really on the case, they couldn't give a shit. Let's be honest, they are probably happy he's gone, probably wished it was one of their own that did it. After all, they tried enough times to get him put away and failed miserably.'

Samir conceded Pepe had a point, but still didn't fancy the alternative. 'It may not have been these three tossers that stabbed your dad, and even if it was, how we gonna find them?' he asked.

'Shouldn't think it will be too difficult. Wally said he's seen one of them a few times – the tall spotty one – coming out of the block of flats opposite the Black Jack. And it was always a Friday afternoon when they came in the pub. He reckoned they had probably come off a building site from what they were wearing – hard hats and boots. Sounds to me like they knock off early for a few pints on a Friday before going home. Doubt if there are that many building sites near the pub. I'll take a gander. If I spot a likely site, then we just hang around on a Friday, and we're bound to spot them.'

'We? Why's it always *we* when you go looking for grief?' whined Samir.

'Because, Sambo, me old mate, you would hate anything bad to happen to me, now wouldn't you?' Pepe grinned.

'Wanna bet?' replied Samir, shaking his head. 'And if and when we do find them, then what exactly are we going to do?' he asked reluctantly.

'We are going to have a little pow-wow, and see if they had anything to do with shoving an eight-inch blade into Ignacio. And if they did, then we are going to knock seven shades of shit out of them.'

'And if they didn't have anything to do with it?' countered Samir.

'Then we'll only knock six shades of shit out of them.'

'Now how did I know you were going to say that?' Samir wearily sighed.

The following Friday, Pepe and Samir were sitting outside the only construction site near the Black Jack pub. It was just two blocks down, a new development of flats. Samir sat staring out the windscreen of the van at the huge estate agents' board nailed to the fence. Eight luxury apartments becoming available in the thriving centre of Peckham.

'Blimey! Who'd pay for a luxury flat in Peckham? They must have to use Paul McKenna to sell them.'

'Peckham ain't that bad,' replied Pepe.

'Peckham ain't that bad? Are you havin' a *bubble bath*?' Samir asked incredulously. 'Name me one place you know that's worse than Peckham, then.'

'Ever been to Basingstoke?' Pepe answered.

'Mmm... you've got a point,' nodded Samir. 'I guess if Hampshire was the arse of the earth, Basingstoke would be right up it,' he grinned.

'Yep,' agreed Pepe. 'And it constantly rains there. And even the birds fly upside down over Basingstoke,' he announced.

'Why's that?' Samir asked.

'Not worth shitting on,' replied Pepe, shaking his head resignedly.

Another hour passed, and a bored Samir started scratching his crotch.

'Everything alright down there, dear?' said Pepe, nodding towards where Samir was furiously clawing.

'What do you mean?' Samir answered defensively.

'I mean, you've been scratching your knackers for the last ten minutes. Pack it in, will yer.'

'Have not!' Samir replied, quickly removing his hand.

'You have! What's the matter? You got a case of galloping knob rot or something?' Pepe accused.

Samir fell silent for a moment, then murmured quietly 'Maybe I have.'

'You what?' laughed Pepe. 'Why? Now what have you been up to?' he asked.

'I saw Chantelle and Chardonnay again last night.'

Pepe shook his head. 'What, those two slappers? I should imagine you're riddled with it then. You wanna get yourself down the clap clinic sharp, my son. Anyway, while we're on the subject, how the hell do you keep them both so happy at the same time?'

'I'm a very generous lover according to them,' boasted Samir.

'Really,' scoffed Pepe. 'And why do they think that?'

'Well, I give 'em nine inches every time I see them,' laughed Samir.

Another thirty minutes passed.

'How long we going to sit here for?' whined Samir,

now becoming very impatient.

'Until we see the three likely lads,' came the stern reply from Pepe.

'Never mind three likely lads, I can see two likely ladies,' whistled Samir. 'Cor blimey, look at the *bacon and eggs* on her,' he said, spying two girls with shapely long legs, both wearing miniskirts, crossing the road in front of the van. 'Wouldn't mind giving them a good *Melvyn Bragg*.'

'Leave it out, Sambo, they're a right couple of munters! Look at the one on the left, she looks like she's chewing a wasp.'

'Any hole's a goal, my son,' smiled Samir.

'Hey, hang on, Sambo, have a look over there,' Pepe interrupted, pointing out three lads coming of the building site. That's got to be them. Clock the tall, spotty one in the middle.'

They watched the three lads walk down the street ahead of them, then hopped out of the van and followed them on foot. The three lads walked past the Black Jack pub, then the tall, spotty one left the other two and crossed the road to enter the block of flats opposite.

'Follow him, see which flat he goes into,' Pepe told Samir. 'I'll see where these two go. You got your phone with you, yeah?'

'Yep,' replied Samir as he crossed the road behind the tall lad. Pepe then followed the other two, who walked on to the bus stop. After a short wait they all got on a bus to New Cross. Then one of the lads got off. Pepe decided to trail him, leaving the third one still on the bus. He followed the lad down a side street to a small terraced house second from the end. Then he called Samir to come and pick him up in the van.

A Question Of Spot

'So what's the plan, Bond?' asked Samir in a terrible Sean Connery accent.

'Don't be a knob, Sambo,' frowned Pepe. 'We wait till it gets dark, and less people around, then we go and give Spotty a knock. Do you think he lives there alone?'

'I would guess so. He let himself in with his own key. It's a bit of a dump.'

'OK, good. Let's go and have a pint at Wally's while we wait.'

Samir nodded in earnest agreement, hoping a drink might give him a bit of Dutch courage.

A little before 8pm Pepe and Samir crossed the road in front of the Black Jack and entered the block of flats. It was a crumbling, five-storey, purpose-built council block that had long since seen its aesthetically pleasing heyday, if indeed it had ever had one. The flat they were heading for was on the top floor and, predictably, the elevator was out of order. They climbed the stairs in silence, Pepe with a dogged determination, Samir with a cautious compulsion. Once outside the front door, Pepe gave it a firm knock. They could hear the television blaring out the *Eastenders'* theme tune. It crossed Samir's mind that anyone who watched *Eastenders* deserved a damn good hiding. There was no answer, and Pepe banged on the door again.

'Alright, alright. Keep your bloody hair on!' came a voice from inside, approaching the door. It swung open revealing a 6 foot 3 inch lad dripping wet from the shower, wearing just a towel wrapped around his waist. Pepe barged through the half-open door, knocking the lad flat on his back.

'What the fu—'

But before he could finish, Pepe had sat across his chest, with his knees pinning down the lad's arms, and given him a hard slap round the face.

'Check the rest of the flat, make sure he's alone,' Pepe called out to Samir, who had hurriedly closed the front door, and now stepped over the two of them to search the kitchen and lounge.

'All clear,' he shouted back to Pepe.

Pepe looked down at his dazed prey, a trickle of blood already dripping from his spotty nose. 'Let's make this quick, with the least amount of pain possible, shall we?' Pepe snarled, and then gave the lad another hard slap for good measure.

'What do you want?' the lad managed to splutter out, fighting to get his breath back, trying desperately to recover from the sudden surprise onslaught.

'Which of you and your tough little mates stabbed that old man from the Black Jack pub?'

The lad stared up at Pepe in complete shock. 'Eh?'

'You know what I'm talking about,' Pepe continued. 'The old man who gave the three of you a good seeing-to. And don't you lie to me, or I'll break your jelly legs.'

'You what?' stammered the lad.

'You heard me, you paralysed piece of piss!' screamed Pepe.

'I don't know nothing about no stabbing. I never stabbed no one,' the lad croaked, a mix of fear and innocence present in his voice.

'Really? Well, that's not what your mate just told us. The one down Union Street. He said you were the one with the blade.'

'What blade? I ain't got no blade. Listen, mate, you've got it all wrong. Yeah, I know the old geezer you mean, but we never did nothing to him.'

179

'Really?' Pepe asked again.

'Yeah, honestly. I don't know what Luke said to you, but that's the truth. I ain't laid a finger on no old man.'

'So what about your two mates, Luke and the other one?' asked Pepe.

'No way,' the lad now managed a half-smile. 'They're way too chicken to do anything like that. Anyway, I thought you said Luke just spoke to you?'

Pepe could see the lad was now recovering his confidence, and decided to apply a little more pressure. He raised his body up just slightly and, keeping his knees firmly on each of the lad's spread-eagled arms, he pushed all his eighty-two kilos onto them, causing the lad to wail out in discomfort. Pepe smiled back down at him. 'Nah, not yet. But we will pay him a little visit once we've finished with you,' he said sinisterly.

'Listen!' the lad pleaded. 'I'm telling you it was nothing to do with us. We heard it was that nutter McCray.'

'Who?' Pepe asked, surprised by this sudden deviation.

'McCray, Finbar McCray! You must've heard of that schizo. He lives down on the Cromwell estate, a right lunatic. His little brother is a chippie on our site. Brain of Britain, he is. The other day he's boasting about how his older bro stabbed the man that killed their father, or some such shit.'

'Really?' Pepe looked up at Samir, who was leaning in the lounge doorway watching them. 'Did you hear that?' Pepe asked Samir. 'Have you ever heard of this Finbar McCray?'

Samir shook his head blankly. 'No, but I know the Cromwell estate. A right warzone. It makes Beirut look like Butlins. Or should that be Butlins look like Beirut?'

he grinned.

With that, Pepe suddenly stood up and motioned to Samir that it was time to leave. They started walking towards the front door.

'Hey,' the lad called, getting to his feet and taking a step after them. 'Who the fuck are you, anyway?' His usual swagger and bravado were returning now that they were leaving.

Pepe turned round and ripped the towel away from the lad's waist as he opened the door. He then reached over and dropped it off the top of the communal balcony, leaving the lad stark bollock naked in the doorway.

'I wouldn't come out here, my son, with no clothes on, you don't want to catch a chill, do you?' smiled Pepe.

'I think he already has,' laughed Samir, nodding down at the lad's rather wretched shrivelled penis.

'Ta-ta for now!' called Pepe over his shoulder, as the two of them strolled away along the balcony and down the stairs out onto the street.

A Ghost From The Past

Pepe rang the number on the card Tel-Boy had given him. Tel-Boy answered the phone straight away.

'Shooters Security. Terry Shooter speaking.'

Pepe laughed at the irony. 'Hi, Terry, it's Pepe, Ignacio's son. Love the name – Shooters Security, that must reassure the clients.'

'Yeah, it wasn't my first choice, but we thought it might deter the thieves, and it seems to be a hit with the clients,' chuckled Tel-Boy. 'Anyway, how are you, Pepe?' he asked, keeping his tone friendly enough, although cursing himself for having given Pepe his number.

'Yep, I'm good, thank you. How about you?'

'Can't complain, just got back from holiday, actually.'

'Oh yeah, anywhere nice?' Pepe asked genially.

'Denver, Colorado, actually. Got a brother that lives out there, so we were staying with him and his family for a couple of weeks.'

'Wow, sounds cool,' said Pepe, keen to keep up the small talk for as long as possible before getting to the real reason for the call. 'A friend of mine was out in Colorado, he said it's beautiful scenery, and great steak country,' he added.

'Yeah? Did he try the *Rocky Mountain Oysters*?' asked Tel-Boy.

'Um… not sure really,' said Pepe slightly confused. 'Why? Are they meant to be good?'

'Well, if you're into that sort of thing,' smiled Tel-Boy. 'They're bull's testicles, actually. Thinly sliced, breaded, and then fried.'

'Cor blimey, did you like them?' Pepe inquired in horror.

'Nah, not really,' laughed Tel-Boy. 'Taste like a load of old bollocks, if you ask me. So anyway, what can I do for you, young man?' he asked, fearing the answer.

'Well, I know you're not keen to drag up the past or anything,' said Pepe delicately, 'but can I just ask you about one name?'

'Well, as I said to you at your dad's funeral, it's all a long time ago now, and my memory isn't what it used to be.'

'Sure, I appreciate that, Terry, and I wouldn't ask unless it was important. It's just that you are the only real link I have with my dad. There's so much I would like to know, but I don't want to be a pain in the arse and keep bothering you,' Pepe said in a sorrowful tone.

'Alright, son, I know. I would like to help you more... Anyway what's this name then?' asked Tel-Boy, feeling a pang of guilt for not wanting to be more cooperative to this bright, likeable young man.

'McCray. Finbar McCray,' said Pepe.

There was a long pause at the other end of the line before Tel-Boy eventually spoke again. 'Your father did know a McCray, back then in the seventies. But it wasn't a Finbar McCray. The one he knew was Charlie McCray. His nickname was Shotgun Charlie. Sorry, don't know any Finbar McCray,' Tel-Boy added.

'Did this Shotgun Charlie have a son?' asked Pepe.

'Yeah, he had a couple of sprogs. Couldn't tell you what they were, me and him weren't exactly close. He just did a few jobs for your dad on occasion.' Tel-Boy was starting to feel uncomfortable. Just hearing that name again after all these years caused him to become slightly ruffled. The memory of that afternoon in Camelot Bookmakers thirty years before came flooding back to him. Shotgun Charlie waving that sawn-off

Purdey around, acting like he was bloody *Scarface*. The truth was, he had been quietly pleased when he heard that they found him with his skull half caved in.

'What happened to him?' Pepe asked.

'Sorry, happened to who?' Tel-Boy asked, returning from his dark secret thoughts.

'Shotgun Charlie? What happened to Shotgun Charlie?'

Another long pause, and then, 'Listen, Pepe, you seem like a real nice lad, and I honestly would like to help you, but... But this is not really the stuff you wanna hear about your dad, believe me. There were a lot of faces back then, none of them any good. You don't want to know about all that bad shit, and if this Finbar McCray is related to Charlie McCray, then stay well clear, alright!'

'OK, OK, Terry, thanks for your time. But is there anyone else I can talk to about my dad. There must be someone else still around who knew him well?' pushed Pepe.

'Well, there was another bloke who used to work with me at your dad's club. His name is Peter Pickles, or Pete the Pig as we all called him. As far as I know, he's got a burger stall down on Clacton pier. You can't miss him, they probably had to build the pier around him. Good luck, my son.' Then before Pepe could say anything more, Tel-Boy had hung up.

A Triple Quarterpounder

'Who knew Clacton had so much to offer,' grinned Samir.

'It's bangin' bro,' agreed Pepe.

'Should've brought your bikini, Dorothy, could've gone for a dip,' laughed Samir.

'You're right, I wish I did. You could have joined me in your gold posing pouch,' Pepe winked back.

'Nah, stopped wearing that now, attracted too much attention. Got myself a new pair of those Aussie Speedos.'

'Really,' frowned Pepe.

'Yep, they call them *budgie smugglers* down under.'

'Mmm... that's attractive,' laughed Pepe.

They walked along the beach front towards the pier, observing those foolhardy enough to brave the freezing waters of the North Sea, jumping in the big ice-cold grey waves. It was a beautiful sunny day, but there was a chilly breeze blowing off the sea, and the majority of the beach revellers were pretty well wrapped up in warm layers, sitting beside their windbreakers, sipping hot tea, determined to enjoy their British holiday by the sea.

'Didn't you once have a bit of crumpet from Clacton?' Pepe asked Samir.

'Can't think of her name now.'

Samir looked blank, shaking his head. 'Don't think so,' he replied.

'Yes, you did. Blimey? what was her name? It was like an old-fashioned name, you know the one? She was all fur coat and no knickers?'

'Hardly narrows it down, does it? Let's face it, Dorothy, most of the totty I've had falls into that category,' laughed Samir.

'True, but this one wasn't quite such a moose. Her dad owned a caravan park down here or something.'

'Ah, you mean Ida. Wow yeah, good old Ida, she was flangetastic!' remembered Samir.

'Ida? Was it Ida?' Pepe questioned, still racking his brains. 'I thought she was Welsh or something? You use to call her another name, what was it?'

'Ida the engine, coz she used to go like a train, the dirty little hussy.'

'Yep, that was it,' laughed Pepe with Samir.

'She couldn't get enough of it,' reminisced Samir. 'She could bonk all day and night that one. Insisted we do it in every single one of her dad's caravans.'

'Kinky cow,' laughed Pepe. 'And did you?'

'Well, we got up to sixty-one, and then she got all freaky on me. She phoned me up one day and told me she was *Keith Cheggers*.'

'You're joking? You got her pregnant?'

'Nah, she was just trying it on. Turned out she was just trying to trap me. Wanted me to get engaged with her, the daft bint. Towards the end, from about caravan fifty onwards, every time we did it, she would ask if I loved her. I just used to say I'm fucking you, aren't I?'

'Bugger me, and they say romance is dead,' laughed Pepe.

'Well, you know what I mean, she was getting all clingy. It drove me nuts, I had to knock it on the head in the end. Shame really, only had another nineteen caravans to do.'

They approached the entrance to Clacton pier and walked through the front archway.

'What's the name of the stall?' Samir asked Pepe.

'Dunno, but Terry said he wouldn't be too hard to

spot, evidently he's a bit of a bloater.'

They continued walking till they got about halfway down the pier, then Pepe spotted him. It was a big double-windowed stall, with the name Pickle's Pies emblazoned across the top. There was a large blackboard on the side listing everything from traditional fish and chips to cockles and mussels. Pepe and Samir walked up to the front and saw a very rotund, red-faced chap, wearing a black apron with *The Codfather* written on it, frying onions.

'Hi there! We're looking for Peter Pickles,' Pepe said to him.

'Well, you just found him, my son, how can I help?'

'My name is Pepe. My father was Ignacio Perez.'

Pete the Pig dropped his spatula on the onions and gave a Pepe a long hard look. 'Are you pulling my plonker, son?'

'No, my mother was Maggie Townsend, and my dad was Ignacio Perez. Terry Shooter told me where to find you.'

'What, old Tel-Boy? How is the ugly bastard? Not as trim as me, I bet.'

'Yeah, he's good. We had a drink together when Ignacio... at dad's funeral.'

'Yeah, sorry to hear about that, my son. I would have come up to the funeral, but didn't know anything about it. I mean, only what I read in the papers. Just what happened to your dad and all that. Bloody shocking, what's the world coming to? Being stabbed on your own front doorstep. I blame the government – not cracking down on all these youth gangs. It was all a bit different in my day, I can tell you.'

'Was it?' Samir interrupted, slightly amused by the fact that this man had obviously forgotten he had worked for one of the most notoriously violent men in England.

Pete the Pig now fixed Samir with a cold glare, then almost immediately softened. 'Probably not. Guess we were all a bunch of scallies back then. Who's cocoa here?' Pete the Pig said to Pepe, nodding in Samir's direction.

'This is my bro Samir,' Pepe did the introductions.

'So, what can I do for you two boys? A couple of quarterpounders and chips perhaps?' encouraged Pete the Pig.

'Actually, I wouldn't mind a pasty,' said Samir.

Pepe gave him a sideways look. 'Actually we just wanted to ask you a few things about my dad.'

'Yeah? No problem, my son. I'll just get your mate here one of my finest pasties, then we can grab a seat and take the weight off,' Pete the Pig said, nodding at one of the plastic table and chair sets in front of the stall. 'Can I tempt you to anything?' he asked Pepe. 'I can recommend the steak and kidney,' he said, patting his ample waistline.

'No, you're alright, just a coffee would be fine, thanks,' Pepe replied.

Five minutes later Pete the Pig joined them at the table, with a piping hot pasty for Samir, coffee for Pepe, and a foot-long hotdog for himself, awash in mustard, ketchup, and fried onions. He saw Pepe clock the size of the hotdog. 'Perks of the job,' he smiled, totally unembarrassed.

Just as he took his first bite, a couple of hot-looking chicks walked past the table. Samir gave them a wink. 'Hello, ladies,' he said.

The two girls turned back. 'Hi handsome!' They giggled in unison.

Pete the Pig, desperate to be included in the flirting, put down his foot-long feast, wiped his greasy hands down his apron and shouted, 'Hey, girls, how'd you fancy a big saveloy?'

'Piss off, you dirty old git,' came the reply, as the girls clattered off in their high heels.

'Oh, bloody charming,' Pete the Pig tutted. 'That's nice, isn't it?' he continued, shaking his head in disapproval. He then called after them, 'Just trying to be civil... Hope you shit yourselves and fall over backwards in it!'

Pepe and Samir looked at each other, and Samir started to get a fit of the giggles.

'Anyway, what did you want to know about your old man?' Pete the Pig asked Pepe.

'Anything you can tell me really,' Pepe replied. 'You see, I only met him once, and that was just a week before he was killed. I don't really know much about him, apart from what they print in the newspapers. Did he have any enemies?'

Pete the Pig burst out laughing. 'Did he have any enemies? That's a good one. Your dad had more enemies than I've had hot dinners.' As he said it, he could see the smile broaden on Samir's face. 'Well, OK, maybe not quite that many, but he wasn't in the business of making friends. During his time he trod on quite a few toes, and he was a heavy man, if you know what I mean? Most people that met him had a lot of respect for him. Either that or they were shit-scared of him. He was a real hard man, not scared of nobody or nothing, he had more *Aristotle* than a Coca Cola factory. Your dad was so tough he could make an onion cry. He had a real presence, when he walked into a room everyone looked round. All the women wanted to be introduced to him, and there were some right beauties back then... None as good as your mum, though. Maggie Townsend, now she was a cracker! Your mum was in the same year at school as me and Tel-Boy. We didn't half fancy her. It was me that introduced her to your dad. Real shame when the two of them broke up. How is she?'

Pepe had already anticipated this coming. 'Unfortunately she passed away a few months back... cancer.'

Pete the Pig shuffled his ample weight uncomfortably in his over-stretched chair. 'Oh shit, I'm real sorry to hear that. You seem to be having it pretty rough recently, son,' he said, with genuine sincerity and sympathy. He finished the last mouthful of his hotdog, and with the aid of his sleeve managed to smudge the grease and ketchup from his lips across his left cheek and down his numerous chins.

'I need to floss,' he announced, while trying to dislodge a piece of onion stuck between his back molars.

'Floss anyone?' he asked Pepe and Samir, who in turn both shook their heads slightly bewildered. 'No thanks,' they replied.

'Be right back,' said Pete the Pig, who managed to free himself from his constricting chair and waddle over towards the fairground rides on the pier.

'I don't believe it,' laughed Samir.

'What?' Pepe asked.

'Have a look at laughing boy now,' Samir said, nodding over to where Pete the Pig was standing. Pepe looked over his shoulder and could see Pete the Pig coming back towards them with a big stick of pink fluffy candy floss in his pudgy little hand.

'You have got to be kidding me?' said Pepe, shaking his head in amazement.

'The man's a complete animal.' Samir had started to get another attack of the giggles.

'I don't know what you're laughing at,' Pepe warned. 'He'll take a bite out of you next. You wanna watch yourself, I bet he loves a bit of black pudding!'

By the time Pete the Pig got back to them, they were both cracking up.

'Hey? Did I miss something?' Pete the Pig asked.

'No, nothing,' Pepe said, trying hard to avoid Samir's eye as Pete the Pig took another mouthful of floss.

'You said Dad had a lot of enemies, can you remember any in particular that would want to actually see him killed?'

Pete the Pig looked thoughtfully at Pepe. 'You sound like the law,' he smiled.

'Well, I guess that's why I ask,' Pepe lied. 'You see, it seems to me that the police don't have much idea who stabbed Ignacio, and obviously anything I can find out to er… help…'

'Well, one name springs to mind straightaway,' Pete the Pig said. 'Vince Connelly. Your dad had a run-in with the Connelly family. Arthur Connelly was a gangland boss up in Birmingham, long since gone now, but his son Vince – a vicious little bastard – had it in for your dad. He went down for a thirty-year stretch, came out just recently according to the papers.'

'Really? Do you think he is capable of doing something like this?' Pepe asked.

'Wouldn't put it past him, but then again he may have come out a changed person. Prison can have quite an effect on a man.'

'Anyone else?' asked Pepe. 'What about McCray?'

'What, Shotgun Charlie? Not unless some bugger dug him up and gave him the kiss of life. He died of severe headache years ago. The rumours were that your old man was behind that. With a bloody great hammer. But he never got pinched for it.'

'What did he and Ignacio fall out about?' Pepe asked.

'It was all to do with the Connelly business. But regardless of that, Shotgun Charlie was his own worst enemy. No one was surprised the day he ended up in the morgue, he was hardly Mr Popular. And if your dad was responsible, then he did a lot of people a favour.'

The three of them sat in silence for a minute or so, all lost in their own thoughts. Then Pete the Pig added,

'The thing is, your dad never did anything unless he had good reason. He only handed it out to those who deserved it. At the end of the day, he was a business man. He ran a very successful kosher business. He had the Bohemia Club, and the sex joints, and some very high and mighty punters. There was that Lord they are all making a big fuss of at the moment – Lord Fitzpatrick. And that slippery new leader of the Tory party – Davenport. They were both close to your dad. I think he did them the odd favour, if you know what I mean?'

Pepe looked puzzled. 'Favour? What kind of favour?'

'Well... you know? Whatever their jollies were, he would accommodate. Getting them prostitutes and the like. Fitzpatrick was partial to young girls, teenage girls. And Davenport, well he was a bit of a fairy, he liked it up the dirt-track, if you know what I mean? Your dad was well connected and could supply most things. Anyway, sorry, chaps, but nice as this is, a little jaunt down memory lane, I really need to get on. Soon be lunchtime, and everyone will be after my pickled eggs.'

He stood up, with the arms of the plastic chair still wedged to his outer thighs. He shook his hips from side to side, allowing the chair to slip free and fall back to the ground.

'Play havoc with your *Nuremberg trials*, these bloody chairs,' he tutted. Then he offered his outstretched hand. Pepe shook it first and thanked him for his time. Then Samir did, and instantly regretted it as he felt the mix of grease and sweat left on his palm. Pete the Pig stepped back into his culinary kingdom, and Pepe and Samir walked away down towards the end of the pier, breathing in the fresh sea air.

'Funny bloke,' Pepe said with a half-smile.

'Funny haha or just funny weird?' inquired Samir.

A Sticky Situation

Pepe approached a group of teenagers hanging round the swings in the rundown children's playground in front of the Cromwell estate.

'Hi. I'm looking for Finbar McCray,' he said.

'What's it worth?' asked one of the more scruffy boys, extinguishing his cigarette butt by stubbing it constantly on the plastic seat of a swing. There were six of them, all around thirteen or fourteen years of age, five boys and one girl. The girl was maybe a couple of years older, and wore all black, with dyed jet black hair, black eyeliner, and black lipstick.

'I just want to know where he lives,' smiled Pepe.

'Information costs money,' said the gobby little kid. 'You don't get nothing for free in this world,' he continued.

'OK, how about I give you a quid, and you tell me what number he lives at?' bargained Pepe.

'A quid! You're a funny man. You can't buy nothin' down the *offie* for a quid,' smirked the boy, the rest of the group all beaming with him. It was pretty obvious that he was their leader, and the rest of them were all trying desperately to mimic his toughness. They were in awe of this young delinquent, apart from the girl, who sat rolling another cigarette, looking bored and uninterested.

Pepe felt in his jeans pocket and pulled out the contents. 'How about three quid, a pack of chewing gum, and a condom?' he offered.

'Go on then,' the boy replied, sticking out his hand.

Pepe gave him the items. 'OK then, which one does McCray live in?'

'Number twenty-one, but I wouldn't bother going

down there. He's never at home,' said the boy.

'Why? Where does he hang out?' Pepe asked.

'That'll cost ya another two quid,' the boy smiled.

'What is this? Daylight robbery? And shouldn't you lot be at school anyway?' rebuked Pepe.

'Don't get arsey with us,' said the boy defensively. 'We weren't doing you any harm. Just sitting here minding our own business till you came along.'

'Flamin' Nora! You're a spunky little thing, aren't you?' Pepe said, causing a couple of the group to snigger.

'What's your name?' Pepe asked.

The boy thought for a moment. 'Caesar… Caesar Tits,' he smirked.

This caused the whole gang to fall into hysterics. Even Pepe couldn't refrain from chuckling with them.

'Alright then, Caesar, if I give you another two quid are you going to tell me where I can find him?'

'Yessum,' answered the boy.

'OK!' Pepe fished out a fiver. 'Give me back the three quid, then,' Pepe said distrustfully.

The boy held out his hand tentatively, with the three coins in it, and snatched the fiver quickly from Pepe.

'He's always down the 24-hour snooker hall, the one on Sullivan Street. Practically lives there, according to my dad.'

'Yeah? OK, thanks. See you around, Caesar.'

'Not if I see you first,' came the reply as Pepe strolled back to his van, and called up Samir.

'Hey, Sambo, how about a game of snooker?'

'Yeah right. Come on, Dorothy, the last time we played you had a right hissy fit.'

'Really?' Pepe asked unconvinced, trying to think back.

'Yeah, I took forty quid off you. Don't you remember? We played for a tenner a frame, and you got all snotty coz you lost the first two, and insisted we played double or quits.'

'You what!' exclaimed Pepe. 'That must be at least three years ago. I've beaten you since then.'

'Not at snooker, sweetheart, you don't know your pink from your brown, but then that's always been your problem,' laughed Samir.

'Alright, alright, choccy bollocks! Tomorrow night after work,' Pepe said. 'I challenge you, best of three for fifty smackers.'

'You're on,' Samir agreed, unwittingly.

The snooker hall was above a large carpet showroom. The entrance was on the street level through a black fire escape door and up a flight of stairs. Halfway up the stairs you could smell the stale air of beer and cigarette smoke. The hall was blacked out and dimly lit. The only light came from the two snooker tables that were in use, the other fourteen stood in the dark. There was a long bar at the top of the stairs, which also stood disused and dingy. The carpet under their feet felt sticky from years of spilt lager and general grime.

Samir glanced across at Pepe as they stood by the bar awaiting attention. 'What a palace,' he grinned.

'Evening, lads,' came a voice from behind a half-drawn curtain at the end of the bar, separating it from a small office. A little bald head popped out. 'What can I get you?'

'Couple of pints of Guinness, please,' replied Pepe.

'Preferably in a clean glass,' added Samir, looking around at the film of ash and grease that seemed to cling to every available surface.

'Coming up,' said the cheery little bald head. 'You having a game as well?' he asked, nodding at the deserted tables.

'Yep, we'll have a couple of frames,' replied Pepe.

'Take your pick,' the little bald head smiled. 'The balls are on the table, I'll switch the light on in a sec.'

The boys took their pints and wandered over to table four. There were a couple of players on table one and a couple on table twelve. The two fella's playing on table twelve were in their late fifties, it was the two on table one that held Pepe's attention. They were maybe four or five years older than Samir and Pepe. Both of them looked pretty rough, but they could certainly play snooker. One of them, the one with ginger hair, had just knocked in a break of thirty-two, so Pepe guessed they were probably regular players.

Samir broke off carelessly, sending six reds back and forth across the table, but fluking a snooker behind the green at the top of the table. Pepe fudged it, and before long he was trailing Samir by twenty-two points.

'This is going to be the easiest fifty quid I've ever earned,' Samir taunted Pepe, who was far too distracted by the players on table one to care. Just then, the ginger-haired one put down his cue and headed for the Gents'.

His mate called after him, 'Oi, McCray, it's your shout, get us a pint on your way back.'

The ginger head grunted and continued to the toilet. Samir heard the name and gave Pepe a shake of the head, 'I might have known,' he said. 'Why else would you bring me to such a dump?'

'It's alright, Sambo, nothing's going to get out of hand. We're just going to have a little chat, that's all.

Samir looked across at McCray's mate, and felt slightly relieved to note that he wasn't a big geezer, in fact he was quite weedy looking.

McCray came back from the Gents', ordered two pints and wandered back to the table. Pepe took a sip from his pint, then nonchalantly walked over to table one, still holding his snooker cue. Samir swallowed hard, and took a few steps closer, but still remained behind Pepe.

'Are you Finbar McCray?' Pepe asked the ginger-haired guy as he was eyeing up a long blue in the top left pocket.

Finbar looked up from his shot. 'Yer mind, mate, I'm taking a fuckin' shot here.'

Pepe ignored this, and coolly asked again, 'Are you Finbar McCray?'

McCray threw his cue down on the table, splaying a group of balls in all directions. 'Yes, I'm fucking Finbar McCray, what the fuck is it to do with you?'

Samir was slightly taken aback by the aggressive nature, but Pepe remained impassive. 'Your father – Charlie McCray – knew my father.'

'Oh yeah, and who's your father? Christmas?' McCray sneered.

'His name was Ignacio Perez,' Pepe said.

McCray walked round the table closer to Pepe. 'That cunt was your father?'

Pepe took a step back, snooker cue tightly clenched in both his hands, positioning himself ready for the expected physical onslaught. But what he did not expect was McCray to pull out a handgun from under his sweatshirt at the back of his trousers.

'I ought to put a bullet in you right now,' spat McCray, waving the gun in Pepe's face.

Samir sprang forward, a surge of adrenalin and nerves racing through his body, unable to stop himself.

'Hey! Hey! Come on, mate. We don't want no *Barney Rubble*, put the *currant bun* down,' he pleaded with McCray.

McCray looked across at Samir for the first time. 'Who the fuck are you?' he shouted. Then, looking back at Pepe, said, 'Has he swallowed a fucking cockney or something?' a thin smile crossing his lips.

'Guns make him nervous,' answered Pepe calmly, managing to conceal his own anxiety. 'I just wanted to ask you a couple of questions.'

'Yeah, and what might they be?' McCray asked, his tone slightly lighter, but the gun still poised in his hand.

'Did you ever see my father?'

'If I did, he would have died with his head blown off, not stabbed by some yob with a penknife.'

'So you had nothing to do with his death?' Pepe asked, his voice quieter, the tension surging out of him.

'Nope, some other fucker got there before me.'

'So how come your little brother is going around boasting that you did it?' asked Pepe.

'Is he?' McCray asked.

Pepe nodded. 'That's what we heard.'

'Stupid wanker! I guess he's just trying to impress his little mates.'

The two of them – McCray and Pepe stood for a while, staring curiously at each other, sizing each other up. McCray had dropped the gun down to his side, and Pepe loosened his grip on the cue. They were studying each other, wondering what it must have been like when their fathers knew each other.

It was Pepe who broke the silence first. 'I have no quarrel with you. Whatever happened between our fathers has nothing to do with us. I'm sorry I interrupted your game, mate. We're gonna leave now, I'd like to stand you a pint on my way out, in respect to your old man.'

McCray nodded, his aggression replaced by respect for his adversary. 'What's your name?'

'Pepe.'

'A pint of Stella then, Pepe.'

'Take it easy, Finbar,' Pepe replied, and walked away towards the bar, with Samir following closely behind, perspiration dripping down his back.

'Can we go home now, please, Dorothy? I don't know about you, but I'm feeling a little light-headed.'

A Time To Reflect

A couple of days later Samir and Pepe were sitting at the top of Greenwich Park by the old royal observatory underneath the impressive statue of General James Wolfe. This was Pepe's favourite place in London, and whenever they were doing a scaffolding job in the vicinity, they would have to down tools at lunchtime and eat their cheese and pickle sandwiches while admiring the amazing view over the Old Royal Naval College and across the Thames to the City of London.

'So now what you going to do, Dotty? You've slapped some poor spotty lad around, whose only crime was to get a good belt from your father before you. Then you scare the shit out of me taking me to a gun fight with a snooker cue in your hand. Isn't it time you dropped all this? Can't you just let it go?'

Pepe put down his sarnie, and took a sip of coffee. 'You're right, Sambo, the other night was a little concerning. I'm sorry. Obviously, I would never have dragged you down there if I'd known he was going to pull a pistol out. But he was never going to use it, morons like that are only full of piss and wind.'

'Bleedin' Nora, Pepe, you never cease to amaze me. I guess you're more like your father than you think. Be honest, weren't you even a little scared?'

Pepe thought for a while, then answered truthfully, 'I think I was surprised more than scared.'

Samir stared at his life-long friend, remembering some of the scrapes they had got into together as schoolboys. In those days it was invariably Samir who started the trouble. He was always the naughty one, the one talking in class, the one being cheeky to teachers, the one playing jokes on the other kids. Pepe was much quieter, allowing himself to be led by Samir. The only time Pepe came to the forefront was when there was a playground scrap. It wasn't because he relished the fight, it was because he felt he always had something to prove. To show that he was tougher than anybody else, because inside he had a hidden secret, and if it ever came out, the other kids might think him weak or sissy. As they got older, the roles changed, and it was Pepe who became the more dominant figure. His unyielding, stubborn character emerging, leaving Samir to be the one that followed. Not that he ever needed much convincing. He would follow Pepe to the ends of the earth. The difference between them was that Samir always knew how far you could go, how far you could push someone, or how far you could stretch the rules. With Pepe there was no such line, he would neither acknowledge nor adhere to any such constraints. And as much as this irritated and concerned Samir, he still felt compelled to go along with Pepe, because the simple fact was that he would do anything for him.

Samir chuckled to himself. 'Do you remember when we were little kids and we built a tree camp each in old Orwell's orchard, in the base of those two huge oaks?'

Pepe smiled as Samir continued, 'I'd finished mine by lunchtime, but you wouldn't let me see yours till you finished. It took you all day, and then eventually you let me over there.' Samir was laughing now as he recounted the story. 'I had just stacked up some old branches and thrown a dirty blanket down on the ground for my camp. I came over to see yours, and it looked more like the Taj Mahal. You even had a couple of your mum's scatter cushions and a curtain hanging inside.'

'Maybe I was just trying to tell you something,' grinned Pepe.

'Good grief! I reckon you were screaming it from the treetops, mate,' Samir chuckled gently. 'Particularly when you pulled out two of your mum's fine bone china cups and pretended to make us a nice cup of tea.' They were both laughing now.

'Don't you think it's bizarre - that same little boy is now picking fights with gun-toting nutcases in billiard halls?'

'I blame the schools,' responded Pepe. 'Four years at Coldingham Upper was enough to turn anyone to a life of thuggery and crime.'

'Yeah… bloody Colditz,' agreed Samir. 'That was a rough school.'

'You're telling me,' Pepe grinned. 'The kids were so ugly, the paedophiles at the gate used to eat their own sweets.'

'So seriously, what are you going to do next?' Samir asked Pepe. 'We can't just keep running around trying to find someone else to accuse of killing Ignacio. Listen, Dotty, I don't mean to sound bad or unsympathetic, but you didn't even know him till a few weeks back.'

'But that's just it, Sambo, I did meet him, I did feel something for him. He had come back into my life, and I was about to know what it feels like to have a dad around for the first time, and then some bastard takes that away from me. If I hadn't met him again, I'm sure I would feel different, but I did, and I feel so robbed now he's gone.'

'OK, sure. You know I'm just trying to understand, yeah?' Samir patted Pepe on the shoulder.
Pepe thought long and hard, before trying to assemble his mixed up emotions into one simple sentence.

'Put it this way, Sambo, how would you honestly feel if someone killed your dad, if they stabbed Winnie?'

Samir looked across the beautiful green park, staring out down the Thames towards the O2 Arena, soaking up the tranquil afternoon. 'I guess I would want to rip their heads off, just like you do.'

A Treasure Chest

Pepe received a phone call from the caretaker/ manager of the sheltered housing block where Ignacio used to live.

'Listen, your dad tended to keep himself to himself. He was polite enough to the other residents, but preferred his own company rather than to socialise or join in with any of the communal activities. The only person your dad was ever really very friendly with was Tom, his next-door neighbour. It was Tom who alerted us to your existence, otherwise we would still be none the wiser. Lucky your dad mentioned that he was meeting you a few days before. Anyway, to get back to the point, Tom has just been in to see me, and he tells me that a few months back, Ignacio asked him to look after an old suitcase for him. He asked him just to keep it tucked away for safe keeping. The suitcase is locked, and Ignacio didn't tell him what was in it, so Tom thought it best not to ask. Well, I guess that as you are Ignacio's sole heir, any property belonging to him should now be in your possession. Do you think you can swing by sometime and collect it? I get the impression Old Tom would like to relinquish responsibility for it as soon as possible.'

'Yes, of course,' answered Pepe, more than a little intrigued. 'I can get over around 4pm today, if that's convenient?'

'Yes, that's no problem. I will have the case waiting for you in my office.'

Pepe got the case home and sat staring at it for five minutes sitting on the living room rug. It was an ancient, small, brown leather case, about 80cm x 50cm. The corners were very scuffed, and dotted around it were several colourful old stickers, including a picture of the Eiffel Tower, Mont Blanc in the French Alps, and the Hotel du Palais in Biarritz. It had two buckle straps, and two locks either side of the frayed broken handle.

Pepe played with the locks, seeing if they would open without the key. But despite their age and condition, they remained securely locked. He went into the kitchen and came back with a couple of screwdrivers and a pair of pliers. He was about to force the lock, but then decided to call Samir first.

'Hey, Sambo, I picked up the case. I wondered if you wanted to come over before I open it?'

'You bet!' replied Samir. 'What do you think is in it?' he said excitedly.

'No idea, probably just some old papers or something,' answered Pepe.

'Or a human head or something,' laughed Samir.

Pepe didn't seem to share the joke.

'Can you hang on for an hour? I'll pick up a few tinnies on the way.'

'Sure,' replied Pepe, wondering to himself if he really could hold on for another hour, the curiosity was already killing him. He sat for another ten minutes just looking at it, before deciding to go and have a bath to pass the time.

Once Samir arrived, it didn't take too long to jemmy the locks, undo the buckle straps and flip the lid open. On the right-hand side was an Aquascutum gentlemen's wash bag. The rest of the case was filled with photos, mainly black and white, and envelopes containing larger photos or papers. The boys sat on the floor beside the case and took a long slug of beer each, before Pepe picked up the wash bag. The weight surprised him, and he placed it down between them. He unzipped it and pulled out a large white handkerchief. Wrapped inside the handkerchief was a polished grey revolver.

'Whoa!' shrieked Samir.

They both stared at it, a cold shudder rippled through Pepe.

'Do you think he shot someone with it?' asked Samir.

'I don't know, Sambo... I don't think I want to know,' said Pepe, quickly wrapping the handkerchief back round the gun and dropping it back in the suede wash bag, as if trying to distance himself from it.

'Come on, let's look through some of these pictures.'

There were a large number of Maggie in her early twenties, and even a few of Pepe as a toddler sitting on the potty and in the bath surrounded by *Matey Bubbles* and yellow rubber ducks. Many of the photos had something written on the back, or a date. There were some pictures of all three of them – Ignacio, Maggie and Pepe on Woolacombe Beach in Devon, and even a couple of Pepe's grandfather – Ignacio's father, on the boat leaving Bilbao back in 1937.

The boys sifted through each one slowly, fascinated by them. There were some photos of Club Bohemia.

'Hey, look at this, Sambo! Do you recognise them?'

Samir took a good look at the black-and-white picture of three men. One was in his fifties, but the other two were much younger, probably in their twenties, with long hair, wearing high-waisted black flared trousers and frilly dress shirts. They were both big men, dwarfing the older fella standing between them.

'That's Terry and Pete the Pig, I reckon,' smiled Pepe.

'Well, grow me some tits and call me Anne Robinson!' exclaimed Samir. 'I think you're right, Dotty.'

The two of them had a good laugh as they went through this batch of pictures. Most of them were of Ignacio, Tel-Boy, Pete the Pig, Harry and Peggy. By reading the scribbled notes on the back, Pepe soon worked out that the old lady at the funeral was the one in the pictures with her husband Harry. There were quite a few pictures of customers in Club Bohemia, dining, or having a drink by the bar. The boys flicked through these a bit quicker, until Pepe spotted a face in one.

'Who's that? I'm sure I recognise him,' he said to Samir.

'Mmm… looks vaguely familiar. Anything on the back?' But there were no notes on this one. The same face appeared in a few more, and then Pepe flicked another one over and saw *Councillor Percy* scrawled on it.

'Look, Sambo.' He passed it across.

'Yes! that's him, isn't it?' Samir got it straight away.

'Percival Davenport. Blimey, who'd have thought he would be hanging out in your dad's club?'

'Yeah, you remember, Pete the Pig mentioned it, said that Davenport and Lord Fitzpatrick use to frequent it.'

'I think I had stopped listening by then, Dotty. I was more amazed by what was going into his mouth than what was coming out of it.'

They cracked open another couple of cans of Bud, and then started opening the envelopes with larger photos in them. It was only then that Pepe realised why Ignacio had wanted to keep the case secret and secure. The photos were all taken in the same large bedroom. It was a very opulent-looking room, with a huge round bed in the middle. The carpet and curtains - thick pile and heavy velvet, in dark reds and maroon. The paintings on the walls – large landscapes in elaborate gilt frames. There was a chaise longue at one end of the room, and an ornate marble table with a lamp, and door to a bathroom on the other side. The photos featured different men in various positions of love-making with an array of naked girls. Pepe and Samir instantly recognised Lord Hubert Fitzpatrick in some of them, due to the recent publicity he had been receiving in the media. There were photos of him with a total of four different girls, all of them very young looking. Pepe and Samir did not know any of the other men caught on camera, until they came across a second collection of photos. This time, it was young naked men in the pictures, and captured in the middle of them was a very engrossed looking Percival Davenport.

Samir let out a whistle. 'Imagine if the press got hold of these?' he said.

Pepe nodded in silence, his mind going into overdrive. It was obvious that these pictures were not taken with their subjects' permission, or indeed knowledge. Therefore there could only be one reason why they were taken. Pepe wondered if Ignacio had decided to use them for blackmailing purposes, and if so, perhaps he had announced their existence to the featured participants just prior to his murder?

A Helping Hand

It was a gloomy overcast Monday morning, and Tel-Boy sat in his office with his feet up on the desk reading yesterday's paper. It was the *Sunday Times*, which he religiously bought with a pack of Hamlet cigars every Sunday morning in his corner shop while they checked his losing lottery numbers for him. He never got the time to read it at home, his weekends taken up with mowing the lawn, taking his and Barbara's cars down the carwash, chauffeuring his two daughters to and from various parties, boyfriends, shopping excursions, hockey matches, and friends' houses. Just when it seemed he had five minutes to himself, Babs would have some other chore for him. It was because of this that secretly he never minded getting up and going into the office on a Monday morning. He would get in nice and early before any of the lads showed up. He would pop the kettle on and make a couple of pieces of toast and marmite in the small kitchenette. Then he'd settle down to a good hour of perusing the Sunday paper.

Old Harry would often spring to mind while he was making his first cuppa. He remembered how Harry always opened Club Bohemia early in the morning, long before anyone else ever arrived and the day's duties of cleaning, ordering and bottling up began. Back then, Tel-Boy used to wonder why anyone would want to get out of bed any earlier than absolutely necessary and go into work. But now he could fully appreciate why that hour or so alone in the morning was so important to Harry. As much as Tel-Boy loved his wife Barbara and the kids, just as Harry did Peggy, it was good to get away from them and spend time in your own space.

In the *Times* supplement section, there was an article about Lord Hubert Fitzpatrick that caught Tel-Boy's eye. The autobiography had been out for a while now. The initial allegations and rumours about some of M'Lord's more sleazy activities had died down due to lack of evidence and some pretty nifty footwork by a high-powered legal firm, whose horrendously expensive services M'Lord had engaged. The high sales of his book were now edging it into the top twenty hardback bestsellers list. But this latest article once again highlighted Dirty Bertie's salacious behaviour. However, unlike the previous column inches of unconfirmed tittle-tattle that had been written about him in the more dubious tabloids, this piece was far better informed and damning. There were references to Club Bohemia and underage girls, and numerous links between M'Lord and the notorious 70s and 80s gangster - The Spaniard. The article finished with a paragraph about the ageing Lord still living the life of luxury between Belgravia and Tuscany, while his alleged long-time friend and sometime business associate - The Spaniard ended up broke, gutted, and filleted on a damp doorstep in Peckham.

The article stuck in Tel-Boy's mind all day. And for some reason his thoughts continually returned to Pepe. Pete the Pig had called him a few days ago saying that Pepe had been down to see him, asking all sorts of questions about who had it in for his dad. It was obvious to Tel-Boy that Pepe wasn't about to sit back and wait for the police to solve his father's murder. And worse still, not only was Pepe looking for the answers himself, but there was a chance that he might take matters into his own hands if he did find the likely culprit.

That night Tel-Boy couldn't sleep. He lay awake all night listening to Barbara's gentle snoring while he wrestled with his conscience. He had promised Babs when they got married back in 87, that he would never get mixed up with the rough stuff any more. She had insisted he cut off all contact with The Spaniard, even though he was no longer even working for him by then, Club Bohemia having been sold off, and The Spaniard spending more time on the Costa Del Crime. However, they had still seen each other every so often, and on the odd occasion when Ignacio needed some extra muscle he would give Tel-Boy a call. But under increasing pressure from Babs, Tel-Boy had to eventually give in, and had stopped seeing Ignacio. What Babs hadn't realised was that the deposit on their first small house had come as a gift from Ignacio. And it was the guilt that Tel-Boy felt at having severed all ties with Ignacio, and the concern he now had for Pepe that was bothering him now. The way he saw it, he owed Ignacio, and there would be no better way of repaying him than to look out for his kid.

The next morning he made the call. They arranged to meet in the Black Jack, which seemed appropriate to Tel-Boy, considering it was Ignacio's regular haunt. Pepe was joined by Samir who was just as intrigued as Pepe by this sudden rendezvous requested by Tel-Boy.

'Listen, son, I'll come straight out with it. I'm worried that you might be heading for a whole shit load of trouble. I'm not here to stand in your way or try and deter you. I can see that you have the same grit and determination as your father, it's written all over you. My worry is that you may end up biting off more than you can chew. No offence, my son, but whoever shoved that steel in your dad meant business. There's a lot of nasty people out there, and unfortunately your dad knew most of them.'

Pepe studied Tel-Boy before replying. 'Thanks for your concern. If you already know I'm not going to give up the hunt for my father's killer, and you've bothered to come all this way to see me, that must mean you intend to help me?'

Tel-Boy allowed a smile of surrender. 'You're as smart as him, too.' He nodded his head. 'I'm not certain that was my real motive. I was thinking more along the lines of helping you stay out of trouble. A guiding hand, as it were.'

Pepe smiled back. 'Well, I'm sure I could use a guiding hand, especially from someone like you, Terry. But I'm curious, why the sudden change of heart or interest?'

Tel-Boy sat looking down at his pint for a few seconds, searching for the right words. 'Because I know your father would have done the same for me if it were my kid.'

The three of them had another couple of pints, and Pepe told Tel-Boy about the contents of the suitcase and his chat with Finbar McCray.

Then Samir bombarded Tel-Boy with questions about Club Bohemia, which had become his latest fascination after seeing all the old photos. They talked about Fitzpatrick and Davenport, before getting onto the subject of Vince Connelly. To Tel-Boy, the obvious suspect was definitely Connelly, but this whole business with M'Lord, the photos, the stories being leaked, and the fact that Tel-Boy knew for certain that Ignacio had received payments in the past from M'Lord, cast a large grey shadow. Maltese Tony's name came up as well, the man Ignacio beat to death in a brawl during the mid eighties in Spain. Tel-Boy didn't know too many of the ins and outs about that. All he knew was that it was the result of a falling-out over the distribution of some of the Brink's-Mat gold. Tel-Boy thought it unlikely that there was any connection between Maltese Tony and Ignacio's death some nineteen years later.

Lastly, Samir asked the question that Pepe had been putting off, uncertain whether he really wanted to know the answer. 'Was the gun in the case the one Ignacio used to kill Brutus and Felix?'

It would be naive of Pepe to somehow convince himself that his father wasn't a murderer, he knew he had to accept that fact. But knowing he might now be in possession of the gun responsible for two of those murders somehow made it all that more real and terrifying.

'I should bloody hope not,' laughed Tel-Boy. 'Your father wouldn't be stupid enough to keep a murder weapon. Nah, I think you'll find the Luger he used on those two is at the bottom of the English Channel.'

'How do you know that?' asked Pepe.

'Because it was me that slung it over the side of the Townsend Thoresen ferry between Southampton and Le Havre.'

The two boys stared at him wide-eyed. Nothing more needed to be said. It was at that point that Pepe understood the loyalty that Tel-Boy had shared with his father.

When they eventually left the pub, it had been agreed that Tel-Boy would dig around on Connelly, find out his whereabouts, etc., while they all pondered what to do about Fitzpatrick.

A Spanish Inquisition

Tel-Boy decided that if he was going to take a drive down memory lane, he should take Pete the Pig with him. He needed an extra pair of hands, and Pete was the only person he could trust with this. With the exception of Babs, no one else knew Tel-Boy's past and who he had worked for. He had purposely kept it a secret from the guys he employed in his security firm and the mates he now spent time with. It could easily cause too much damage should it ever get out, in particular affecting his business. While Joe public was fascinated with underworld characters like The Spaniard, to the extent that they even made them cult heroes, by and large the vast majority would feel very uncomfortable doing business with his known associates.

He and Pete the Pig picked up Pepe and Samir outside Samir's place in Camden, and before long they were joining the M1 and picking up speed towards the Midlands, going after Vince Connelly. The memories of doing the same journey thirty years ago with The Spaniard, Pete the Pig, and Shotgun Charlie came flooding back to Tel-Boy. Truth be known, he hadn't been half as much worried back then as he was this time around. Maybe it was age, maybe it was the different company. Back then he was in his mid twenties, full of confidence and courage. He'd never backed down from a fight, no matter who the opponent was. And working for The Spaniard, he'd had to take on quite a few hard bastards in his day. Not so much when he was on door duty for the club or the sex joints, that was all fairly straightforward – chucking the odd drunk

215

out who got a bit lairy, or banging a couple of punters' heads together if they couldn't behave themselves. That was all in an average night's work. But it was when The Spaniard asked him to do extra duties, outside of the normal business hours, that the heat turned up. Collecting bad debts, leaning on suppliers, and frightening off any competition. All these activities invariably required more than just a slap. And unlike the mugs in the club or the sex joints, a lot of these Herberts were usually tooled up and quite menacing. It wasn't unusual for Tel-Boy to come up against iron bars, baseball bats, even motorcycle chains. And on more than one occasion he had found himself staring down the barrel of a gun. But back then he took it all in his stride. He was handsome, young, fit, and strong. He knew he could handle himself, plus he had the added protection of The Spaniard being by his side, which was no small advantage. Now here he was, thirty years later, about to do it all over again. But this time his hair was receding, he had a substantial midriff paunch and a dodgy back. He glanced at his fellow passengers, Pepe, Samir, and good old Pete the Pig. OK, Pepe and Samir were still young guys, capable of taking care of themselves, but Pete was hardly in the best of shapes. He started to wonder whether this was such a great idea. It was hardly the same as having The Spaniard sitting next to you.

For the first half of the journey, Pete the Pig had been amusing them with his endless jokes.

'Hey this is a good one for you, Tel-Boy,' as he started to crack another one. 'You'll like this, it's bloody funny. Did you hear about the Chinese godfather?'

'Nah,' came the rather weary reply from Tel-Boy.

'He made them an offer they couldn't understand,' snorted Pete the Pig. Samir fell into fits of laughter, whereas Tel-Boy and Pepe just allowed themselves an appreciative grin. Both were too lost in their own troubled thoughts, thinking about what might lie ahead. Samir and Pete the Pig then started playfully arguing about the six nations rugby championship. England had just narrowly lost their first two matches, to Wales by two points, and then to France by one point. Samir was trying to remain enthusiastically upbeat as usual, talking up England's strengths and their potential to improve. However, he was on a hiding to nothing. There was no denying Wales were in fine form, having beaten England, annihilated Italy, and finished off France at home in Paris. And to make matters worse, Pete the Pig was taking the side of the Welsh. He claimed to be more Welsh than English because some cousin of his had once had a knee trembler with Neil Kinnock. Samir's conviction started to wane in the face of Pete the Pig's triumphant Welshness, however obscure his claim was, and the car eventually fell into silence.

Pepe sat staring out of the window, his mood quiet and tense, his feelings mixed. On one hand, he had high expectations that he was at last about to meet his father's killer, but by the same token there was an overwhelming feeling of dread, in case it turned out to be true. It had been different with the lads from the building site and Finbar McCray. Pepe hadn't stopped to think when he went after them. Maybe in the back of his mind he had already doubted they were responsible, and that the action he was taking was just to confirm what he already knew. Maybe he was just letting off steam, looking for the nearest person to pin some blame on. But this was something else, something completely different. Vince Connelly was a well-known hardened criminal, and someone with a real grudge against his father. Finbar McCray possibly had good reason to be mad with The Spaniard, but the truth was, he had no certainty that it was he who had killed his father - Charlie McCray. There was never a case against The Spaniard for his murder, no evidence ever found, in fact, no suspect ever arrested for the murder of Shotgun Charlie. Vince Connelly, however, had just spent the last thirty years behind bars because of The Spaniard. Now how much more motive would someone need? But even when the police had given him a right good grilling following Ignacio's stabbing, Vince's alibi stood strong, and after twenty-four hours down the nick he was released. The alibi being that he was working in a restaurant that night. The constabulary knew the restaurant was owned by a friend of Vince's, which made it somewhat dubious, but two witnesses confirmed that he was there all evening, and currently there was no cause − suspicious or otherwise − to dispute this. That may have been good enough for the police, but it wasn't good enough for Tel-Boy and Pepe. And in a couple of hours' time, when they had arrived at the restaurant, they intended to take over where the police had left off, but it wasn't going to be a grilling, more an inquisition, a Spanish inquisition!

An Offer He Couldn't Refuse

It was around 9pm when they arrived at Giuseppe's Sicilian Pizzeria in Moseley, a couple of miles out of Birmingham city centre. The restaurant had a car park at the back, and Tel-Boy brought the powerful Bentley Brooklands to a stop up close to the fire doors that were open – revealing a very large, sweaty-looking chef, puffing on a roll-up, and beyond him the kitchens.

'Evening, Chef,' nodded Samir in greeting, as they walked past him back round to the front of the restaurant. A grunt came from the chef as he flicked his butt end across the car park and lumbered back into the kitchen.

'How many Michelin stars does this place have again?' chuckled Samir as they entered the front. Inside, the restaurant was a throwback to the 80s. It seated forty covers on two rows of five tables of four up each side. The tables themselves were covered with bright red gingham check cloths, and each held a large green Carlsberg ashtray and a straw-wrapped chianti bottle, complete with candle in the neck, and five years of dirty dried wax on the sides. Covering the walls were large faded pictures of the Gulf of Palermo. At the opposite end from the front door was a small bar, with steps down to a small office behind it, a swing door to the kitchen, and a door on the right leading to the toilet. There was a family of four sitting at one of the tables, but the rest were all unoccupied. Tel-Boy and the others settled for the table nearest the front door.

A man in his early forties of Italian origin appeared from the kitchen, and brought over some menus for them. 'Evening, gentlemen,' he greeted them. 'My meatballs are off, and the dish of the day is Pasta Carbonara.'

'Do you offer an all-you-can-eat-type deal?' asked Pete the Pig.

'I'm afraid not,' came the somewhat bemused reply.

'Mmm... What size do your pizzas come in, then?' frowned Pete the Pig. The waiter, who the group had now assumed was the owner - Giuseppe, gave Pete the Pig a taut smile, similar to the smile his Mafioso grandfather from Sicily used to give people before he slit their throats.

'I'm sure sir will find them more than generous,' he assured Pete the Pig. All four of them then settled for a pizza, plus an additional pasta side dish for Pete the Pig, and Giuseppe strolled back to the kitchens to give chef the orders.

'You think he's here tonight?' Pepe asked Tel-Boy.

'Can't be certain, but if my tip-off is correct, he is here every week night. Evidently he is living in the flat above.'

'How did you find out about this place?' asked Samir.

'I've got a pal on the force – Barry Sykes. He checked the records after they took Vince in for questioning. He's not a bad bloke for a copper, old Sykes. He was just a Detective Constable when I first met him back in the 70s. His boss was a right bastard – DCI Eddie Mullins, or Edward the Confessor, as they used to call him. Him and your father got on alright, though,' Tel-Boy nodded at Pepe.

'Why did they call him Edward the Confessor?' asked Samir.

'They reckoned he was the master of interrogation, but that was mainly due to his unorthodox technique.'

'What was that?' inquired Pepe.

220

'He kicked the shit out of you,' smiled Tel-Boy. 'Nobody ever left the interview room before confessing. Ten minutes with him, and Mother Theresa would come out swearing she was a serial killer. Eventually the force managed to retire him off, he left under a cloud of corruption charges, which unsurprisingly all fizzled out, and no action was ever taken against him. But Sykes ain't like that, he's one of the good guys. He's made it to superintendent now, down in the Met.'

'Does he know why you wanted the information on Connelly?' asked Pepe, getting a little concerned that the police might know exactly what they were up to.

'Yep, but I made a deal with him. If we find out that Connelly was behind your father's death, then we let him know, and pass it over to the police to deal with it.'

'What happens if he's not, but we've already roughed him up a little?' asked Pete the Pig.

'Sykes ain't interested in that. The likelihood of Vince going bleating to the police is nil, and even if he did, Sykes says they'll turn a blind eye on it. Scum like Connelly are not exactly high on their Christmas card list.'

The pizzas arrived, but this time the waiter was English, in his mid fifties, but still lean and very fit looking. Tel-Boy recognised him instantly. The blond hair was now greying, and he was carrying a few extra pounds since his twenties, but the mean-looking face was still the same. The lips were thin and wet, the nose long and flaring out, the eyes cold blue, shadowed by the long thick, almost mono eyebrow, and lastly the deformed looking left ear, or the remainder of it. Tel-Boy nodded at Pepe, and all four couldn't help but stare at Vince's back as he walked away from the table.

'How we going to handle this?' Pepe asked Tel-Boy.

'Might as well enjoy the grub, wait for the other table to leave, then have a little word in his shell-like,' answered Tel-Boy.

By the time the occupants of the other table had left, and the four of them had finished their pizzas and paid the bill, it was 10.30pm. Vince was back in the kitchen, and Giuseppe was down in the little office. Pepe and Samir went out of the front, and walked round to the back of the restaurant to the open fire doors in the car park. Just as they got there, two teenage lads – the kitchen porter and the commis chef – came out, chatting and laughing in Polish, on their way to the bus stop. Pepe took a swift peek inside. He could see it was just Vince and the big chef left inside. He sent a text to Tel-Boy, who had been waiting in the front of the restaurant. Now he and Pete the Pig got up from their table, and walked to the kitchen. As they came through the swing door, Pepe and Samir came in the back.

'Hey, this is kitchen! Not for public!' shouted the chef. It was only then that Vince took a good look at Tel-Boy for the first time that evening.

'Hey, don't I know you from somewhere?' he asked Tel-Boy.

'Cast your mind back thirty years, and you might remember. I worked for The Spaniard. How was Belmarsh?' Tel-Boy asked with a mocking smile.

'Why, you fuckin' arsehole!' screamed Vince, picking up a steak knife. 'I'll cut your fuckin' balls off.'

'You'll need a bigger knife than that, pal,' said Tel-Boy, psyching himself up for an assault. Just then Giuseppe appeared from the office, running into the kitchen.

'Hey! What's going on?'

But before he could get an answer, Pete the Pig stuck his foot out, tripping Giuseppe and sending him crashing to the floor. At that moment all hell broke loose. Vince rushed at Tel-Boy, blade first. The chef went to Giuseppe's aid, but was blocked by Pepe and Samir. Vince's steak knife tore into Tel-Boy's left forearm as he fended it away, and he gave Vince a whopping right punch, square in the middle of his face. The bone in his nose shattered and blood pissed out. Pepe and Samir were having trouble containing the chef, who had grabbed an overflowing chunky glass ashtray and given Pepe a good smack on the side of the head with it. Pepe, completely dazed, with a large gash above his right eye, was now having trouble staying on his feet. The chef still had hold of him by the throat, and in a fit of desperation, Samir picked up a cast-iron frying pan and gave the chef a good wallop on the head with it, looking like something from a Tom and Jerry cartoon.

Giuseppe had attempted to get back on his feet but Pete the Pig had used his ample weight to knock him back down, and was now binding his hands with an extension cord lying on the floor. With the chef unconscious, Giuseppe tied-up and gagged with a disgustingly soiled dish cloth shoved in his mouth, Pete the Pig and Samir were now free to help Tel-Boy sweep the stainless-steel worktop clear, and pin Vince spread-eagled down on it. Pepe was out of it, slumped on the floor trying to staunch the flow of blood from his temple with a towel.

The adrenalin was pumping through Tel-Boy now, the forgotten brutality from his past emerging once again after years of being dormant. He grabbed hold of a butane torch. 'You've heard of crème brûlée? Well, this is cock brûlée. Undo his trousers, Pete,' barked Tel-Boy.

Samir held down Vince's arms, and Tel-Boy his legs, while Pete the Pig ripped down his pants.

'What the fuck are you doing? What the fuck do you want, you crazy bastard!' screamed Vince. Tel-Boy fired up the flaming torch and grabbed hold of Vince's testicles, twisting them violently in his hand.

'You have anything to do with The Spaniard's stabbing?' Tel-Boy shouted.

'No, I fucking didn't!' shouted back Vince.

'Mmm… I'm not sure I believe you,' said Tel-Boy, shaking his head, hovering the flame a few inches above Vince's dangly bits. 'Are you sure?' he asked again.

'Yes, I'm fucking sure. Do you think I'm stupid enough to wanna go back inside?'

'Well, I think you're fucking stupid, but I guess you could be right about prison,' conceded Tel-Boy. 'Tell you what, I'll make you an offer. Tell me the truth and I won't set light to your prick, but if I think you're telling me porkies, I'll shove this torch where the sun don't shine.'

'I am telling you the fucking truth, you cunt,' spat Vince.

'Well, that's not very polite. Don't get Mr Snippy with me,' Tel-Boy chided. 'You know what? I think I will set light to your privates anyway.' And with that, he let go of Vince's bollocks and flashed the flame across his pubic hair. Vince let out an agonised yelp, as his thatch went up in smoke and the skin beneath it scorched and frazzled.

Samir started to feel a little nauseous at the sight of this, and threw a glass of water over the blaze, leaving a deep pink scald.

Vince's mouth was frothing with spittle as he yelled, 'You fucking madman, I told you I had nothing to do with it. I ain't interested in The Spaniard any more. I did thirty fucking years, I just wanna get on with what's left of my life.' He was almost in tears now, blood and snot streaming out of his nose, phlegm and spit dribbling down his chin.

'Let him loose then, boys,' said Tel-Boy, extinguishing the torch. He went over and helped Pepe to his feet.

'Come on, son, our work here is done.'

They backed out of the kitchen, leaving Vince sobbing, and the chef starting to come round.

'How's that head?' Tel-Boy called over his shoulder as he slammed the Bentley's magnificent 6.75 litre engine into drive and accelerated out of the car park towards the M1.

Samir checked Pepe's cut. 'It don't look good. I think he should have some stitches.'

'Let's just get out of here,' said Pepe quietly. 'I'll sort it back in London. I just wanna go home.'

'OK, son,' said Tel-Boy, 'but we'll go via Luton Hospital. It's literally just off junction eleven.'

He then turned to the passenger seat, grinning like a naughty schoolboy, 'You alright, Pete?' Tel-Boy checked, 'Just like the old days. Did you have fun back there?' Pete the Pig looked back across at Tel-Boy.

'Yeah, I'm OK. But to be honest, I didn't think much of their pizzas. I mean it's not a proper pizza unless it's got anchovy on it.' Tel-Boy started to giggle, and before long Samir and Pete had joined in, the previous hour's tension releasing from them.

A Headache

'Hello, handsome!' greeted Samir.

Pepe nodded in return, then immediately regretted it, as the intensity of the dull ache above his eye increased.

'Whoa! That's quite a scar you're going to be left with there,' said Samir, eyeing up the twelve stitches starting from Pepe's hairline and running down his right temple.

'Gee, thanks, Sambo. Did you come here to cheer me up?'

'Of course I did, Dotty. I even bought you some chocolates,' smiled Samir as he passed Pepe a half-eaten box of Ferrero Rochers.

'Hungry, were you?' Pepe frowned.

'Got stuck in traffic, didn't I? Felt a bit peckish. Anyway, how are you?'

'So so,' answered Pepe. 'But can't seem to do much. If I do a lot of moving around I feel sick and get dizzy spells. The doc says I should just stay put in bed for a couple of days, and he's given me some strong painkillers.'

'Well, just do as you're told for once,' said Samir reprovingly. 'We don't need you back at work for a week, so just take it easy.'

'Thanks, bro, I will then. I just feel so out of it at the moment. I could quite happily stay in this bed for a month.'

'That bad, huh?' asked Samir.

Pepe confirmed with a faint smile. 'Listen, I can't really remember much about what happened up in Birmingham. The last thing I recall is that crazed chef coming at me. What the hell happened?'

'He gave you a right crack with a glass ashtray. You were obviously concussed.'

'And then?' Pepe queried.

'Well, then yours truly – the main man, the hero of the hour – came to your rescue, and knocked him clean out with a frying pan,' gloated Samir.

'Yeah, alright, Butch. And then?' repeated Pepe.

'Well, then we pinned down Connelly, and Tel-Boy decided to set light to his ging-gang-goolies. And as he lay there, with his short and curlies going snap, crackle, and pop, he managed to convince us he had nothing to do with your dad's stabbing.'

'You think it's true?' asked Pepe.

'Believe me, Dotty, he was more than convincing. The risk of going back inside was more than ample deterrent for him not to do anything stupid like attack your dad. He had cracked up by the time Tel-Boy finished with him. He's certainly not the supposed hard case that he used to be.'

Pepe closed his eyes.

'Hey, you alright?' asked Samir anxiously.

'Yeah, I'm fine. I guess it's all over now,' sighed Pepe.

'What do you mean?' asked Samir. 'What's all over?'

'Well this whole thing with Ignacio, we've come to a dead end now.'

'Not really,' argued Samir. 'What about Lord what's his face? I thought you and Tel-Boy had come to the conclusion that your dad was blackmailing him?'

'Lord Fitzpatrick is dead,' whispered Pepe.

'Hey? When? What happened?' Samir asked in astonishment.

'Have you not seen the news this morning?'

'Nah, mate, been too busy rigging up the scaffolding for that Hammersmith job.'

'Lord Hubert Fitzpatrick died at home last night. A heart attack, evidently. Guess all the recent strain must have got to the old boy in the end. With him gone, it's unlikely that we will ever find out what went on between him and Ignacio. Maybe the police will dig something up, but there's nothing more we can do.'

The two of them sat in silence for a few moments.

'So does that mean we can put all this to rest now?' encouraged Samir hopefully.

'I thought you were enjoying it, Butch,' winked Pepe.

'It had its moments,' grinned Samir. 'But we're a couple of scaffolders, not the bleedin' Sweeney. I'm sure the law will catch up with whoever stabbed your dad eventually. Let's leave it to the professionals... and I don't mean Bodie and Doyle,' laughed Samir.

'Maybe you're right, Sambo, maybe you're right,' Pepe resigned exhausted.

A Body To Die For

Percival Davenport woke up full of the joys of spring. It was a beautiful bright morning, the birds were chirping merrily, even the dustbin men were whistling a joyful tune. Everything seemed to be going his way. His party had rallied behind him, making him the most popular Tory leader since Thatcher's heyday. They were creeping forward in the polls, proving that once again the Conservatives were serious contenders for power after such a long bleak period in opposition. The recent thorn in his side had been removed when they reduced Ignacio Perez to a pile of ash in an urn. And to top it all off, that disgusting old imbecile Fitzpatrick had just dropped down dead, burying all incriminating links between himself and The Spaniard.

All day long, Percival was unable to wipe the idiotic grin off his face. Some of the other members of the house were heard to comment that he looked even more smug than usual, if that was at all possible.

One Lib Dem MP went even further when he asked, 'What on earth has got into Davenport? Or should I say who?! Maybe he's been out on the scene with Mandy all night.'

But Percival was oblivious to any such mockery. Nothing could dampen his high spirits, which were only enhanced further when he snorted a line of coke. A line that he had expertly arranged on the front cover of his favourite and well-thumbed copy of *Latino Jocks* magazine before leaving Westminster. He then screeched out of the commons car park in his gleaming Lotus Esprit and joined the few remains of the evening's rush hour, the majority of commuters having already left the capital, homeward bound to suburbia and beyond.

The remaining light of the day was fast disappearing as Percival cruised down the embankment towards Chelsea, the lights of Lambeth, Vauxhall, Chelsea, Albert and Battersea bridges twinkling before him, as he propelled the Esprit forward, like a rocket past the other motorists. Bearing right, leaving the Thames behind and heading towards Ealing and his impressive five-bedroomed home overlooking the common, he felt on top of the world. He wanted to go and celebrate, the familiar urge to be reckless was rearing its ugly head again. The thought of going back to an empty house was far too depressing. He gunned the twin-turbocharged engine, hitting 60mph in a smidge over four seconds, flying down Finborough Road and entering Earls Court. Ten years earlier he used to love hanging out in this area. Old Brompton Road was a great place for an evening out. A light dinner and a bottle of Rioja at Balans, a couple of pints in the Coleherne, *with the leather all around,* ending up in Bromptons, for a groove, or a last-ditch attempt at picking up a bit of trade for the night.

So it was no surprise that Percival suddenly found himself slowing down and turning off, searching for a parking space. Before long he was parked and walking down Old Brompton Road, approaching the Coleherne. As he neared, he came to a halt, pausing for a moment.

'Is it really such a sensible idea for the leader of the opposition party to go waltzing into a well-known gay leather bar and order a Campari and soda? Probably not, even if you are off your tits on coke,' Percival chuckled to himself. He strolled leisurely past the pub, trying with little success to catch a glimpse inside through the high blacked-out windows, framed nicely with hanging baskets full of pink geraniums.

At the corner of Finborough Road he stopped and muttered, 'Fuck it! It might even get me some more votes.' He then turned and walked purposefully back into the pub and ordered a pint before he changed his mind again.

The bar was reasonably busy and dimly lit, so that very few of the clientele seemed to notice his arrival. After all, he looked just like any other city suit, cruising for a bit of rough. He stayed at the end of the bar, trying to keep a fairly low profile, while still keeping an eye out for any good-looking Joes. The first pint went down a bit too quickly and, rather than nurse an empty glass, he ordered a second. Halfway through it, a stocky big-built man in his late forties, wearing motorcycle leathers approached him at the bar.

'Hey, how you doing?' he nodded as he took up a leaning position on the bar next to Percival.

'Hi, very good. And you?' Percival replied, in a friendly but nonchalant fashion.

'Yeah, not bad. Busy day at the office?' he asked Percival, giving him a wink as he did so. Percival wasn't sure whether it was a conspiratorial wink, confirming that he knew who Percival was, or just a friendly gesture.

'Yes, I thought I would treat myself to a well-earned drink. And you? What do you do?' Percival asked.

'I'm a courier,' he replied.

'Ah, hence the leathers, and I thought it was just to excite the wolves,' smiled Percival, gesturing around the room at the other patrons.

'Well, a bit of both, I hope. And does it?' he asked Percival.

'Does it what?'

'Does it excite you?' the courier asked, slowly caressing the large schlong lengthening in his leather pants.

'It's certainly caught my attention,' smiled Percival. 'How about another drink?' He indicated the courier's empty glass.

'Sure. Need a piss first, though.'

Whilst the courier was not exactly Percival's type, he was pleased to share the company of an amicable stranger. Over the years, the types of men that Percival found he was attracted to had changed considerably. As a younger man, he had always preferred the youthful, pale and under-nourished looking twinks. But as he had got older, his tastes had also matured. He still desired younger men, at least ten years his junior, but now he lusted after real beefcake. Solid, muscular types, fit and rugged. The courier wasn't a bad-looking bloke, but he was a bit too old, and fell more under the category of beer belly than bench press. In fact, Percival hadn't considered him in the least bit sexually attractive until the courier had taunted him with his enlarged endowment. But as Percival ordered him another Stella and waited for him to return from the toilet, his glance fell upon something far more appealing. Leaning against the slot machine was an Adonis. Younger and taller, a Grecian God, athletic as Apollo, as tempting as Dionysus. With long dark hair, and penetrating, seductive eyes. To say Percival was smitten was an understatement of colossal proportion. He was spellbound, bewitched, mesmerised.

The courier returned, ready to finish what he had started, the cool but purposeful seduction of Percival Davenport, future prime minister. But it was too late,

Percival's attention was otherwise engaged. After chatting for another ten minutes with barely a grunt in response, the courier glanced over his shoulder to see what Percival was staring at so intently. He quickly realised that he was being sidelined and it was time to move on.

'Well, thanks for the drink. Give Tony and Cherie a kiss next time you see them,' he said, trying to make light of his obvious rejection. And he wandered off to the other side of the bar, leaving Percival so entranced in his hypnotic stare that he hardly noticed the courier leaving.

The Adonis finished his drink and, making sure Percival was observing his every move, he went to the door, turned back to Percival, flicked a look of encouragement, and went out into the night. Percival hurriedly finished his pint and followed him out of the door. The Adonis had crossed Finborough Road and was walking slowly towards Brompton Cemetery. He turned and looked back at Percival, smiling, before he continued with his walk. When he got to the locked gate of the cemetery, he stopped again, glancing around to make sure no one was observing. He smiled again at the approaching Percival, then scaled the railings with ease, and dropped into the graveyard beyond. By this time Percival had nearly caught up with him, but had difficulties getting a decent foothold and hauling himself over the railings in pursuit. He managed to make it, but ripped the knee of his pinstripe trousers. Not that he cared, his heart was thumping, the overpowering excitement filling his whole body with delirium.

Once over the wall, Percival made his way down the central path. The further he walked from the main entrance, the darker it became, as he left behind the bright street lights. About fifty metres down, he noticed a white shape to his right. In the darkness he could make out the Adonis's white vest, and he followed him into the middle of a group of elaborate ancient headstones and tombs. Adonis was leaning against one, with his belt unbuckled and his jeans undone. Percival went to him, a surge of electricity thundering through his body as he caressed the younger man's chest. They embraced, and their lips locked in a long sensual kiss, their tongues probing, searching deep inside each other. Percival removed the white vest, exploring, licking, caressing, fondling every inch of the young man's strong, defined, smooth torso. He dropped to his knees in front of the open jeans, nuzzling his face in the warm, hardness contained in the snug-fitting white briefs. Slowly he eased the jeans down, leaving them unravelled around the ankles. Using one hand and his tongue, he unleashed the thick, rigid manhood and guided it greedily into his mouth. It didn't take long before the climax came. The Adonis arched his back, thrusting his rock-hard shaft even further into Percival's mouth, who gratefully consumed and guzzled the hot sticky fluid that ejaculated with such force. After making sure every last drop had been slurped up, Percival reluctantly withdrew his mouth from its prize and looked up.

'What's your name?' Percival asked.

'Nikolai.'

'Well, Nikolai, you were just what I've been looking for,' Percival smiled up at the handsome, chiselled face.

'And you were exactly who I've been looking for,' came the reply, as the heavy rock crashed down on Percival's head. For a moment Percival remained still, the blood slowly emerging from under his hairline, trickling down his face in several rivulets. Then he slumped sideways, twitching violently, staring up at his slayer.

'That's for Dimitri. For what you and that bastard Spaniard did to my brother. It's taken me a long time to catch up with you two.'

Percival's face was now awash in blood. Nikolai brought the rock up above Percival's head for a second time and then let it come slamming down again. The twitching subsided, and what had begun as a perfect day for Percival ended as his very last.

www.ingramcontent.com/pod-product-compliance
Lightning Source LLC
Chambersburg PA
CBHW030106030726
47498CB00007B/2278